"You're a low-d

Penny accused, jabbing a finger into Sam's rock-hard belly.

"A coward?" the fearless cop repeated incredulously. "Just what exactly am I supposed to be scared of?"

"Me," she announced without hesitation.

Sam's spirits sank. So, he thought with a sigh of resignation, she had him pegged. Even before he'd realized it himself, she had guessed that he was falling in love with her, the little brat. Correction. The grown-up, incredibly sexy little brat.

What Penny apparently *hadn't* grasped quite yet was one simple fact.

He had absolutely no intention of doing anything about it.

Dear Reader,

Welcome to Silhouette Special Edition . . . welcome to romance. We've got six wonderful books for you this month—a true bouquet of spring flowers!

Just Hold On Tight! by Andrea Edwards is our THAT SPECIAL WOMAN! selection for this month. This warm, poignant story features a heroine who longs for love—and the wonderful man who convinces her to take what she needs!

And that's not all! *Dangerous Alliance,* the next installment in Lindsay McKenna's thrilling new series MEN OF COURAGE, is available this month, as well as Christine Rimmer's *Man of the Mountain,* the first story in the family-oriented series THE JONES GANG. Sherryl Woods keeps us up-to-date on the Halloran clan in *A Vow To Love,* and *Wild Is the Wind,* by Laurie Paige, brings us back to "Wild River" territory for an exciting new tale of love.

May also welcomes Noreen Brownlie to Silhouette Special Edition with her book, *That Outlaw Attitude.*

I hope that you enjoy this book and all of the stories to come.

Happy Spring!

Sincerely,

Tara Gavin
Senior Editor

Please address questions and book requests to:
Reader Service
U.S.: P.O. Box 1325, Buffalo, NY 14269
Canadian: P.O. Box 1050, Niagara Falls, Ont. L2E 7G7

SHERRYL
WOODS
A VOW TO LOVE

Silhouette®

SPECIAL ▼ EDITION®

Published by Silhouette Books
America's Publisher of Contemporary Romance

For Diane Kay McDaniel, who had the wonderful idea
of bringing Sammy and Penny together.
This one's for you.

 SILHOUETTE BOOKS

ISBN 0-373-09885-5

A VOW TO LOVE

Copyright © 1994 by Sherryl Woods

This edition published by arrangement with Harlequin Enterprises B. V.

Printed in U.S.A.

Books by Sherryl Woods

Silhouette Special Edition

Safe Harbor #425
Never Let Go #446
Edge of Forever #484
In Too Deep #522
Miss Liz's Passion #573
Tea and Destiny #595
My Dearest Cal #669
Joshua and the Cowgirl #713
*Love #769
*Honor #775
*Cherish #781
*Kate's Vow #824
*A Daring Vow #854
*A Vow To Love #885

*Vows

Silhouette Books

Silhouette Summer Sizzlers 1990
"A Bridge to Dreams"

Silhouette Desire

Not at Eight, Darling #309
Yesterday's Love #329
Come Fly with Me #345
A Gift of Love #375
Can't Say No #431
Heartland #472
One Touch of Moondust #521
Next Time . . . Forever #601
Fever Pitch #620
Dream Mender #708

SHERRYL WOODS

lives by the ocean, which, she says, provides daily inspiration for the romance in her soul. She further explains that her years as a television critic taught her about steamy plots and humor; her years as a travel editor took her to exotic locations; and her years as a crummy weekend tennis player taught her to stick with what she enjoyed most—writing. "What better way is there," Sherryl asks, "to combine all that experience than by creating romantic stories?"

Sam Roberts and Penny Hayden
request the honour of your presence
as they exchange their marital vows
at two o'clock in the afternoon
on Saturday, the twenty-fifth of September
at Whitehall Episcopal Church,
Boston, Massachusetts

Prologue

In the eyes of sixteen-year-old Penny Hayden there was something a little dangerous and very exciting about the handsome young man standing beside her grandmother in the streaming sunlight at the front of Boston's Whitehall Episcopal Church. Though he was wearing an expensive suit made of the finest Halloran fabric and tailored to fit perfectly, he looked as if he would have been more comfortable in ripped denim and black leather. His blond hair had been newly trimmed and was slicked back, but it was still an inch or two longer than any respectable teen's in her conservative private school back in California.

Of all the new relatives she was meeting for the first time at the christening of six-month-old Elizabeth

Lacey Halloran, Penny thought Sam Roberts was by far the most fascinating. She had been drawn to him from the first instant she'd seen him. At the same time, the unexpected intensity of her reaction was something entirely new and faintly puzzling. Frankly, it scared her silly.

Sam's exploits, at least as told by her grandfather, had taken on almost mythic proportions in her mind, adding to his intriguing aura. Every time the stories were told, her parents managed to look faintly alarmed, as if they'd guessed right off what her reaction to Sam would be. She'd probably been half prepared to fall head over heels in love with him before she ever got to Boston just because he was the kind of boy they'd always placed strictly off limits. At sixteen, she figured she was long overdue for both a rebellion and a gigantic crush. That probably explained why she trembled inside every time she set eyes on him.

Unfortunately, Sam Roberts, who'd just turned nineteen, hadn't so much as glanced at Penny the entire weekend. In fact, he'd stood on the sidelines at most of the family gatherings this weekend, looking a little lost, a little lonely. She knew with some gut-deep instinct that he would never admit to either of those feelings. He probably didn't even recognize them.

Penny could empathize. She still felt like an outsider with the tight-knit Hallorans. For one thing, they all lived on the opposite side of the United States. None had visited them in Los Angeles, despite her grandfather's overtures. She guessed they were still as shocked as her family was by the discovery that Penny's mother Ellen was the daughter Brandon Halloran had never known he had.

Personally, Penny thought it had been incredibly romantic the way Brandon Halloran had tracked down her grandmother Elizabeth and then discovered the truth. Penny had been dying to go to Boston for their long overdue wedding, but everyone had agreed it would be best if only her mother and her Aunt Kate were there for the first meeting of the two sides of the family. She'd had to wait six months, for this christening, to get her first look at all these intriguing new relatives.

Because of her own tumultuous emotions she could guess how Sam must be feeling. It made her want to reach out to him. To her parents' regret, she'd been picking up strays most of her life, always befriending the outsiders in her class and in her neighborhood. It looked as if she might carry the trait into adulthood.

Right now, though, Sam was in the center of things, caught up in this special celebration. He, along with Penny's grandmother, had been chosen as godparents for the firstborn in the fourth generation of Hallorans.

Sam's expression was solemn as he listened to the minister explain his responsibilities. Only when he glanced down at the baby, still being held in her mother's arms, did a look of absolute delight and reverence soften his features. Penny saw her grandmother reach over and squeeze his hand and wished like crazy that she could have been the one standing up there beside him, sharing this special moment in a family where tradition meant so much.

Later, at her grandfather's house, Penny watched with her heart in her throat as Sam awkwardly cradled the baby in his arms. She told herself she was being silly and romantic, but she fantasized that it was their baby he was holding with such a look of tenderness on his face. Then she wondered when she had turned into such a nut case. She'd always been the steady one, the precocious one. She'd never fantasized about anything until this week . . . when she'd seen Sam Roberts for the very first time.

"What are you thinking about so seriously?" her grandmother asked, coming up beside her and giving her a squeeze. "You've been awfully quiet all weekend. It's not like you."

"They're a little overwhelming, don't you think?" Penny admitted aloud for the first time.

Elizabeth Halloran gave her a conspiratorial grin. "That's exactly the way I felt when Brandon introduced me to them for the first time, but it doesn't last. Pretty soon you'll feel like one of the family." She followed the direction of Penny's gaze. "Quite a hunk, isn't he?"

Embarrassment flooded Penny's cheeks. She hadn't realized she'd been so obvious. "Who?" she asked, hoping to save face.

"Sam."

"I guess," she said with a disinterested shrug.

"He's older than you are, though."

"Not that much. A couple of years."

"But he had a much tougher life. He grew up a lot faster."

"Is he going to go into business with grandfather?"

"That's what Brandon wants and Kevin and Jason don't object. Sam started working in the company right after his sister Dana got involved with Jason. He seems to have a real aptitude for sales and marketing, but according to your grandfather, Sammy's gotten it into his head he wants to do something on his own. Maybe he's feeling overwhelmed by all the Hallorans, just like you. How come you haven't asked him about this yourself? You've never been shy."

"I've never met anyone like him before," Penny admitted. "He seems so mature compared to the guys in school. Whenever I get around him, I get all tongue-tied."

Her grandmother regarded her with disbelief. "Now that has to be a first. How come when I was seeing Brandon, you had so much to say? You sounded very wise and grown-up."

"All talk," Penny retorted. All the textbooks in the world on human sexuality and family relations hadn't prepared her for the giddy, off-kilter way Sam Roberts made her feel.

Her grandmother grabbed her hand. "Come on. I'm sure he's tired of hanging around all these grown-ups, too. Maybe the two of you can go to a movie or something."

Humiliated by the thought of being foisted on Sam, Penny held back. "Grandmother, no. You can't make him take me out."

"Going to the movies so you can get to know someone from out of town isn't the same thing as a date, for goodness' sake. Besides, I won't have to *make* him do anything. One thing you'll learn as you get older is that subtlety goes a long way. Now watch a pro in action."

Determinedly tugging Penny along in her wake, Elizabeth Halloran breezed through the throng until they were standing beside Sam.

"Hey, Mrs. H., how're you holding up?" he asked with genuine affection. He didn't even glance at Penny.

"I'd give anything to kick off these shoes, but Brandon would be appalled," Elizabeth Halloran confided.

Sam shot her a knowing look. "Come on. You know Granddad Brandon thinks you walk on water."

"I won't be able to walk at all, if I stay on my feet in these shoes much longer. I don't know why I let him talk me into these three-inch heels at my age."

A devilish hint of mischief in his eyes, Sam leaned down. "He probably told you they made you look sexy."

To Penny's astonishment, a girlish pink tint flooded into her grandmother's cheeks. She winked at Sammy.

"As a matter of fact, he did," she admitted. A familiar glint of determination sparked in her eyes. "By the way, Sammy, weren't you telling me earlier that the new action movie, the one with that Arnold person with the huge biceps, is playing now?"

He regarded her innocently. "You want to see it?" he inquired. "We could sneak out."

"Not me," she said with a laugh. "But Penny was telling me that she'd been dying to get to it. She's seen all of his films, isn't that right, dear?"

"All of them," Penny confirmed, her gaze fastened on Sam's incredible blue eyes, trying to read his reaction to her grandmother's ploy. She might not be all that experienced, but it sounded less than subtle to her. And it was pretty clear that Sam hadn't mistaken her intentions, either. He finally looked at Penny as if she'd just appeared magically at her grandmother's side.

"Maybe we could go before you go back to California," he said right on cue.

Sam hadn't said it like a man who would die if she said no, but he had said it. Penny felt her heart begin to race. "That'd be great. I'd really like to."

Sam nodded, meeting her gaze directly for the first time. "I'll get back to you." He leaned down to kiss her grandmother on the cheek. "Gotta run. I've got a date."

When he'd gone, leaving Penny trembling with an odd mixture of anticipation and a first-ever attack of jealousy, her grandmother beamed at her. "Now, see, that wasn't so difficult, was it?"

"Do you think he'll really take me?"

"He said he would, didn't he? I've never known Sam to go back on his word. Now, come on. Let's go have some of that fabulous cake Dana just cut."

For the next few hours Penny's excitement mounted until she barely slept a wink all night. But as the remainder of her stay with her grandparents wore on, Sam didn't call. Nor did he stop by. Slowly she began to realize that he never would. The *date* had been no more than a polite gesture, not a promise at all.

However, on her last night in town, he appeared at the door just after her grandparents had gone out for their favorite after-supper ice cream. This time he was dressed in jeans and a T-shirt and a leather jacket that added to his mystique of danger. He looked exactly as she'd envisioned him. Penny's heart began to thud wildly. She sensed she was about to embark on something that would change her life forever.

"Sorry I didn't get back to you, kid. It's been a busy week. You want to catch that movie tonight?"

Despite his failure to call, despite the rudeness of showing up at the last minute, Penny was thrilled and thoroughly disgusted with herself because of it. One thing every girl in her class knew was that appearing anxious killed a guy's interest. Unfortunately, she hadn't the vaguest idea how to act aloof when she could hardly wait for whatever the night held in store.

"I'll change. It'll only take a minute," she said at once, thinking of the outfit she'd planned, the one that would make her look more grown-up in his eyes.

"You look fine," he said automatically, without even giving her a glance. "Besides, we'd better get going if we're going to make the show."

Disappointed to be going out in an old pair of shorts and a faded blouse that she'd worn to help her grandmother in the garden rather than in the sexy sundress she'd anticipated wearing if this day ever came, Penny didn't argue. She jotted a note for her grandparents, then followed him to his car. She told herself the important thing was to be going at all. She'd never felt so grown-up before in her life.

When Sam didn't say another word all the way to the theater, Penny struggled for conversation. Silence or halfhearted replies met most of her attempts. Her ego tumbled further when he bypassed the popcorn and soda without even asking if she wanted anything.

Inside the darkened theater and filled with romantic yearnings, she imagined his arm around her shoulders or his hand brushing hers. Instead he remained slouched down next to her, his eyes glued to the screen. She told herself he was only being a gentleman.

The slights, however, were beginning to add up. During the silent ride home, when he never once suggested stopping for a hamburger or a soft drink, she began to get angry, really angry. Even the lowest form of creeps back home offered a snack at the end of an evening. The evening she'd been dreaming about with so much hope was turning out to be a dismal failure.

The fact that she was still attracted to Sam despite his behavior only made her angrier.

"Why'd you take me to the movies?" she asked, finally summoning some of the spunk she was famous for.

He glanced over at her with a surprised expression. "You said you wanted to go."

"And being a dutiful member of the family, you forced yourself to show up, right?" she snapped, infuriated by his patronizing attempt to place the blame for this miserable evening on her. "Next time, don't do me any favors."

"Hey, Granddad Brandon said . . ."

Penny thought she might very well die right where she sat. "You talked to my grandfather?" she asked in a low, hurt voice.

Now, at last, he did look at her. "I talk to him every day," he replied evasively, but guilt was written all over his handsome face.

Oh, God, it was worse than she'd thought. Angry at Sam, at her grandfather, but mostly at herself, she lashed out. "And what exactly did he say to you? Did he tell you that I was moping around the house, that I had this silly crush on you and you should give me a break and spend a couple of hours with me? Maybe give me a little thrill, so I can take the memory back to L.A.?"

Something in his expression changed and before she knew what he'd intended, he'd pulled to the side of the road, turned off the ignition. "Is that what you want from me? You want a little thrill? No problem." His hand circled the back of her neck and drew her toward him.

Penny's heart thundered so hard she was sure it could be heard clear to L.A. She wanted to protest as he lowered his mouth to cover hers, but the words snagged somewhere in the back of her throat.

There was nothing tentative or tender about the kiss. It was a bruising, punishing clash of wills and it sent a dark, throbbing, sensual thrill right through her, just as he'd promised. She thought she heard him groan, but then she was lost to the wildly provocative sensation of his tongue invading her mouth. For the first time in her life, she began to understand all the excitement about sex as an unfamiliar heat spread through her, tempting her beyond reason.

Then she remembered that the man making her feel this way didn't care about her, that this kiss meant nothing to him, that he was merely delivering what she'd asked for and she burned with humiliation. He had awakened her sexuality, but in the process the fragile flowering of her self-esteem was crushed.

Pushing him away, she retaliated with more anger and sarcasm.

"Tell grandfather he owes you extra for the kiss. I'm sure it's worth more than the fifty bucks he probably paid you for your time."

Sam couldn't have looked more stunned if she'd slapped him. He muttered an oath under his breath as he visibly tried to bring his temper under control.

"Okay, let's just wait a minute here," he began in a more placating tone.

By now, though, Penny was in no mood to listen. "No, you wait a minute, Mr. Smart Guy Roberts. I don't need any of your favors." She reached into her purse and snatched out a five-dollar bill and threw it at him. "That ought to cover the gas. As for you, your company isn't worth spit."

There was something gloriously energizing about releasing all her pent-up anger and frustration. She seized the opportunity to fling open the car door and leap out. She was halfway down the next block before he could get to her. He pulled alongside.

"Get back in here."

"Not if my life depended on it."

"Granddad is going to kill me if I show up without you."

"That's your problem, pal."

"Penny, look, I'm sorry. It's not what you think, I swear it."

The halfhearted apology came too late. She turned and drew herself up, realizing that in the past couple of hours she'd grown up more than she had in the previous sixteen years.

"Go to hell, Sam Roberts," she said in the quietest, most dignified voice she could muster.

And then she cut across a lawn where he couldn't follow and ran the rest of the way home.

Later, as she cried herself to sleep, she thought her heart was broken. It was several, miserable months later before she finally chalked the entire incident up to experience. At least she had learned at an early age that no matter how badly you wanted to, you couldn't make another person fall in love with you.

She'd also learned, or so she told herself repeatedly, that anyone as insensitive as Sam Roberts wasn't worth loving at all.

Sam watched Penny stalk away from him, her thin shoulders thrown back, her head held high, and thought he'd never met anyone quite so infuriating.

Or as fascinating, he added with regret. She was going to grow up to be a real hell-raiser and a real beauty on top of that. Even at sixteen there was something about her that made a man's blood race in an entirely inappropriate way. He never should have kissed her, but he hadn't been able to stop himself and it had only made matters worse. She was furious and he was hot and frustrated.

Hell, he'd wanted to kiss her from the first moment he'd set eyes on her, but he'd placed her off limits. With her privileged background, she was the kind of girl who deserved the best, and Sam Roberts hardly qualified. Everyone knew he was the kind of guy who'd break a girl's heart.

He thought of the hurt he'd seen in Penny's eyes when she'd realized that her grandfather had set up this movie thing and wondered if he'd made a terrible mistake in giving in to Brandon's coercion. Then he considered the way she'd battled back and decided that, hurt or not, Penny Hayden would always be able to take care of herself. Too bad he wasn't going to be around her to watch the fireworks.

Chapter One

At first glance, primarily because of his size, the man lurking in the shadowy hallway of Penny Hayden's apartment building looked faintly alarming. Penny immediately tried to quiet the little tremor of fear that zigzagged down her spine. The man was standing in plain sight, after all, not hiding like a dangerous criminal.

He probably had a very good reason for being there, Penny decided. Maybe he was just locked out and waiting for the landlord to turn up with a key. Or maybe he was meeting someone and he'd arrived early. Those were certainly logical explanations, and she much preferred those to the violent scenarios that had flashed through her mind when she'd first spotted him.

Of course, she reminded herself as she moved down the hall with slightly more caution than usual, she did have a tendency to be entirely too trusting. It came from growing up with doting parents who'd always made her feel safe and protected. They had fueled her natural curiosity about the unknown, rather than instilling fear.

That, of course, was precisely the reason Brandon Halloran had insisted she take a self-defense class before moving from Los Angeles to Boston, where she'd be entirely on her own for the first time in her life. He'd determinedly tried to plant the idea in her head that every stranger represented danger, which was ridiculous, of course. Strangers were just people whose fascinating secrets she didn't know yet.

On the off chance that just this once her grandfather might be right, Penny drew in a deep breath and marched past the man without her usual sunny smile. She kept her gaze straight ahead, but alert for any sudden movement, even the slightest shift of his eyes in her direction.

Unfortunately, she had terrific peripheral vision. In addition to tracking his movements, she also noticed his well-muscled physique, emphasized by a tight, faded black T-shirt, and the shaggy blond haircut beneath a backward Red Sox cap. The look was scruffy, but definitely sexy.

There was something vaguely familiar about the lazy half smile that turned his expression into something far more dangerous than she'd first recognized. Intent on mayhem or not, men with smiles like that were lethal to the quiet, studious existence she'd promised herself for the next two years. They disrupted peace of mind without even trying, to say nothing of what they managed to do to pulse rates. Women were drawn to men like that the way moths were attracted to flames. She'd always figured the deadly futility in both instances wasn't an idle comparison. She steeled herself against becoming a victim.

"Don't you know you should beware of strange men who're just hanging around in dark hallways?" he inquired.

Penny's stomach clenched, more at the patronizing tone than out of fear. Her feminist hackles rose. Of course, she knew that. Did the man think she was an inexperienced idiot? There were definite ways to correct that impression. She considered several of them, then dismissed them just as quickly. Maybe he hadn't meant to taunt her. Maybe he was like her grandfather, unable to resist any opportunity to give advice.

Penny flashed him a tentative smile. He responded by falling into step beside her. Warning signals began to flash and that prickle of unease she'd dismissed came back as a full-fledged case of panic. Just in case her grandfather knew more than she did about Boston's lowlifes, she tried to recall something—*anything* from those self-defense classes. For instance, exactly how and when should she make her self-protective move? It definitely should be before the guy followed her inside her apartment, which she was more and more certain was his destination.

She spent ten nerve-racking seconds considering her strategy, debating whether it was even called for, then decided it would be sheer stupidity to take any chances. She whirled, slammed one booted foot into his shin and aimed her denim-clad knee at his groin. It didn't exactly connect, but she was satisfied with having proven her point, anyway.

Filled with confidence and adrenaline, she reached for an arm, expecting to flip him onto his back as easily as she had her instructor. Big as he was, this guy wasn't nearly as beefy as Karate Todd. Her hand clamped around a wrist. Not two seconds later, she had one arm pinned behind her and she was locked against a body that was all male and seemed to be shaking with indignation. Or was it laughter?

Penny listened and heard the telltale snicker. The creep was actually laughing at her. Fury replaced fear, along with the firm conviction that she could handle the situation, no matter how out of hand it seemed to have gotten. Grateful that she was wearing her Western boots, she raised a foot to crunch the daylights out of his instep, only to find herself unceremoniously tossed over his shoulder.

"Next time, don't pick on somebody bigger than you are, short stuff," he advised as he plucked her apartment key from her hand and headed unerringly for her door.

How the devil had he known which apartment was hers? she wondered. Had he been stalking her? She'd read about stuff like that. In Los Angeles it happened to celebrities all the time. Usually, though, the person being stalked was someone famous or at least had a passing acquaintance with the stalker. She'd never seen this idiot before in her life. She surely would have remembered anyone with a voice that reeked of smoky sensuality and unbridled amusement—a combination she found particularly irksome under the circumstances.

Of course, given her humiliating, upside-down position with all the blood rushing to her brain, it was a strain remembering her own name. She did manage to recall a prayer or two. Unfortunately, she had a hunch she was going to need more than prayers to get out of this. Even more unfortunately, every single thing she'd learned in that self-defense class had suddenly flown out of her head.

She was, however, thinking clearly enough to make one firm decision. She knew absolutely that she was not under any circumstances going into her apartment with this man, even if that meant she had to scream her head off to catch the attention of her brand new neighbors. Which, now that she thought about it, was what she should have been doing long ago, instead of trying to convince herself that she was in no danger.

She opened her mouth and let out a bloodcurdling yell that would have done Tarzan proud. It was greeted by an equally vocal string of obscenities from her captor and the satisfying sound of doors opening up and down the corridor. She followed up with one more ear-shattering scream, just to prove that she meant business.

"You little twit," the man muttered, jamming the key into her lock and flinging open the door.

To her astonishment, he turned around, faced down all the neighbors and said, "Just a little lovers' quarrel. Don't mind us."

It didn't take much to imagine his smile and that amused, patronizing tone charming the daylights out of all of them. "It is not—" she screeched emphatically, only to have the words cut off by the slamming of the door behind them.

It took a supreme effort, but she convinced herself that no one could possibly be fooled by his lame remark, that even now police cars were speeding to her rescue.

Hopefully, he wouldn't kill her before they arrived, she thought just as she was dumped in a sprawling heap onto the sofa. She glanced up. Indeed, the expression in his eyes was filled with murderous intent. For the first time she stopped being mad and started to get just the teensiest bit nervous.

Maybe Brandon and everyone else had been right to worry about whether she knew what she was getting herself into by moving to Boston. She found the unfamiliar flash of self-doubt extremely irritating. No, dammit! A twenty-five-year-old woman had every right to follow her own dreams. If that meant burying herself in a stuffy laboratory at Harvard while she pursued a thesis for her Ph.D. in English, she couldn't imagine why it was anyone else's concern.

Some women preferred to concentrate on intellectual pursuits that might one day make a difference in society. Some women just weren't cut out for romance. Look at her Aunt Kate. Well, that was a bad example. Aunt Kate had been a strong, independent, powerful lawyer. Now she carried a diaper bag in addition to her briefcase. Talk about ruining an image! Tough talk and baby talk were incompatible, it seemed to Penny. But the way Aunt Kate used to be . . . now there was a role model. Why couldn't her mother and especially her grandfather, Brandon Halloran, see that she wasn't burying herself in a lab because she was afraid of life?

Someday, though, they'd be proud of her when she was off in Sweden or Switzerland or wherever it was that they handed out the Nobel prizes. She hadn't quite decided yet if she wanted the award to be for curing cancer or for literature. It occurred to her that quite possibly that was why her entire family was in such an uproar.

She could just imagine their reaction when they heard about some damnable man invading her apartment during her very first week in town. That thought gave her the bravado to launch another attack on the unsuspecting man, who was staring out the window, probably to make sure that the police weren't rolling in before he finished up whatever mayhem he intended.

Without hesitating to consider the consequences of riling him further, she bounded across the room. She leapt up, looped her legs around his waist and one arm around his neck in what she thought was a fairly effective choke hold. To her astonishment and regret, he shook her off as if she were no more than a pesky nuisance.

"Do that again and we're going to have one serious problem on our hands," he warned.

He muttered something more under his breath. Penny'd always been taught that whispering in the presence of others was downright rude, but she was relatively certain that she should be glad in this instance that she hadn't heard what he'd said. If the furious sparks in his eyes were anything to go by, she had a feeling he hadn't been welcoming her to Boston.

Sam Roberts stared pensively out the window and tried to get a grip on his temper. He had grown up tough, always lashing out furiously and without thought. It had kept him in hot water most of his adolescence. Raised by his sister, he'd rebelled against everything. It sometimes astonished him that Dana had put up with all his garbage—defending him, bailing him out of trouble, loving him. For her sake, he'd finally learned to control the temper that was currently being put to an extreme test.

He struggled to stay calm as he considered the promise that had gotten him into this fix, a promise made to Brandon Halloran, the man who'd really turned his life around. Granddad Brandon had treated him with the kind of respect that a man felt compelled to earn. He owed the old man. So when Brandon had called a few days earlier and asked just one thing of him—that he look out for Penny Hayden—Sam had no choice but to agree, even though his last experience with the kid hadn't ended so well.

The role of undercover cop-turned-baby-sitter didn't appeal to him, but a debt was a debt. He was beginning to see why Brandon had thought the brat needed someone to watch out for her. Apparently she thought she was invincible. She'd scrapped with him as if she considered it an even match. She didn't need a baby-sitter. She needed an armed guard.

Not that Sam entirely trusted Brandon's motives. The old man had a habit of meddling in the lives of everyone he cared about. He'd even been making noises about it being about time that Sam found himself a woman to smooth out his remaining rough edges. What twenty-eight-year-old Sam had told him was succinct and hopefully threatening enough to snuff out any matchmaking ideas the old man might have had.

But this thing with Penny had surfaced a little too conveniently for his liking. He would do it, though, because he'd learned one important lesson from the Hallorans: families always stuck together—and the Hallorans had made him one of their own from the instant Jason Halloran had married his sister. Today was the first time in a long while that he'd regretted the family ties.

Unfortunately, at the moment he had an even bigger regret. He hadn't noticed the precise instance when Penny's supreme self-confidence had slipped away. He'd never meant to scare her to death. In fact, he had actually thought she'd recognized him. That smile of hers had certainly been friendly enough. Not until she'd attacked him had he gotten the message that she'd panicked, thinking that a stranger was about to harm her.

Dammit all, as a cop who dealt with crime victims all the time he should have had better sense. He could have calmed her with a word or two, just by the mention of his name, in fact. Although, given the way their last encounter so many years ago had turned out, she might have attacked him, anyway. Instead, though, he'd reacted as he would have in the old days, instinctively fighting back rather than being ruled by his head. His lack of sensitivity grated. Apparently he was doomed to getting it wrong whenever Penny was involved.

Just as he figured that the day had gotten just about as bad as it could get, he heard the sound of sirens and realized it was about to get worse. The guys at the station weren't going to let him live this down anytime soon.

Muttering another oath under his breath as they pounded up the steps, he strode over to let them in. He wished belatedly that he'd taken the time to clear up this misunderstanding before their arrival. Unfortunately he'd been afraid to open his mouth, fearful of what would come out.

He had to admit, though, that he took a sort of grim satisfaction in the prospect of watching Penny Hayden stumble all over herself to explain why she'd called the cops on her own relative, albeit one only distantly related by marriage,

The first cop up the stairs, taking them two at a time, gun drawn, was Ryan O'Casey. He was followed by his burly, African-American partner, Jefferson Kennedy Washington, who was called that only by someone who had a death wish. He was J.K. or Jake to his colleagues on the force.

Both men froze at the sight of Sam. "You just get here?" Ryan asked. "What's happening inside?"

"What's happening inside is that this cretin manhandled me, broke into my apartment and probably intended to kill me," an indignant voice said quite calmly from a point slightly above Sam's elbow.

Sam had forgotten exactly how tiny Penny Hayden was, or maybe it was his own belated spurt of growth and years of weight training that made her suddenly seem small. The way she'd taken him on in that hallway told him size wasn't something she worried about. He swore again and tried to ignore the amusement that immediately crowded the worry straight off both men's faces.

"You picking on the little people again, Sam?" Jake demanded, looking Penny up and down approvingly. "You know Ryan hates it when you do that."

"Very funny," Sam retorted, scowling at the whole lot of them.

Penny glanced from one policeman to the other and apparently didn't like what she saw. "Aren't you going to arrest him? Put some handcuffs on him?"

"I doubt that'll be necessary, miss," Ryan said politely. He glanced pointedly at the gathering of neighbors in the hall. Every single door had been flung open. "Maybe we should take this inside, see if we can't straighten it out."

"Good idea," Jake said.

"I do not want this man in my apartment," Penny informed them, trying to block the way. "I want him locked up in a cell so that he can't harm other innocent citizens."

"Oh, give it a rest," Sam snapped as he lifted her aside, then marched over to the unopened bottle of whiskey he'd spotted on the kitchen counter and poured himself a stiff drink. He held up the bottle. "Anybody else want one?"

"We're on duty," Jake reminded him. His gaze narrowed. "Thought you were, too."

"Nope. I'm taking the rest of the day off. I consider it a hazardous-duty benefit."

Penny was regarding them all suspiciously. "What's going on here?"

"Well, ma'am, that's what we'd like you to tell us," Ryan said.

He said it in his most courteous tone, Sam noted. He and Jake made a good team. Ryan soothed, while Jake tended to make suspects quake in their boots without ever opening his mouth. He just loomed over them.

"Sam here is a police officer," Ryan explained softly. "I'm guessing he must have been here on a stakeout. Is that right, Sam?"

"Something like that," he agreed.

Penny's mouth gaped. "A policeman? Sam?" Something that might have been comprehension flickered in her eyes. An interesting shade of red crept up her neck and into her cheeks.

"Sam Roberts?" she said weakly, sinking onto the sofa.

He lifted the glass in her direction. "Nice to see you again."

"Oh, hell," she murmured.

He took considerable satisfaction in seeing her day disintegrate right before his eyes. He figured that made them just about even. Granddad Brandon, on the other hand, still had to pay up big time.

Chapter Two

Penny surveyed the man standing in her minuscule kitchen from head to toe. Now that he was in the light and fear wasn't clouding her vision, she could see it was Sam Roberts all right. Taller, broader through the shoulders and sexier, if that was possible.

Now she knew why her pulse had skipped at the sound of his voice. She'd heard it often enough in her dreams. That's what came of adolescent fantasies. On rare occasions, they stretched clear into reality to zap common sense.

One thing for sure, his outrageous behavior hadn't changed a bit. He was living up to everything Penny remembered about him from their brief but memorable encounter at the christening of his niece, Eliza-

beth Lacey Halloran, firstborn in the fourth generation of Hallorans. For an entire weekend he had
blatantly regarded Penny as a pesky adolescent,
hardly worthy of his attention.

Back then she had chafed at being so summarily
dismissed, especially by the first true love of her entire life. The one kiss they shared still burned in her
memory. The whole thing had been humiliating and
ridiculous. Forever after, she had told anyone who
asked that she couldn't stand the smart-mouthed jerk.
She'd finally started to believe it herself in the past
couple of years. There were times when she couldn't
even remember what he looked like.

Well, that much was obviously true, she thought,
thinking of the terrible mistake she'd made in that
hallway.

Of course, she had also told herself that Sam Roberts's being in Boston had nothing to do with her decision to come to Harvard after years of self-imposed
exile from the East. Judging from the way her heart
was thudding at the moment, she'd been lying
through her teeth about that, too. Apparently some
things never changed.

Today, despite his obvious and acute embarrassment in front of his colleagues, he'd managed to
maintain that same insolent, arrogant attitude. His
entire demeanor suggested that she was totally at fault
for the mix-up. Even now he was lounging against the
kitchen counter, a drink in hand, while she stumbled
all over herself trying to explain how she'd confused
one of Boston's finest cops with a common criminal.

Penny drew in a deep breath and tried to reclaim some sense of dignity. "It was dark. Besides it's been a long time since we've seen each other, over nine years in fact. He was dressed in a suit and tie at the time and looked considerably more respectable than he does at the moment," she said.

Now she allowed her gaze to linger on his disreputable attire to emphasize the point. There was the very last time she'd seen him, of course, when he'd been dressed more casually, but he hadn't looked as muscular back then. It was amazing what a little weight training could do to an already sexy body. She blinked and looked away. It wouldn't do to spend too much time thinking about that.

"On top of that," she said finally, "he never called me by name, never introduced himself. What the hell was I supposed to think when this jerk tosses me over his shoulder and hauls me into my apartment? It's not a technique used by any welcoming committee I've ever heard of."

Jake and Ryan listened sympathetically. All the while their eyes sparkled with merriment. They were clutching their sides, probably to keep from laughing out loud. No doubt it was Sam's sour expression alone that kept them from howling.

"Look, I'm not the one who ought to be on trial here. Cop or not, he broke in," she accused irritably.

"Do you want to file charges?" Jake inquired.

Judging from the expression of expectancy on his face, he really wanted her to do it just for the fun of it. Penny could just imagine how Sam, much less the rest of the family, would react. Still, she had to admit to being tempted. She could get even for a lot just by saying yes.

"I suppose not," Penny finally said with some reluctance.

"Thanks, brat," Sam said with that increasingly familiar edge of sarcasm. "Don't do me any favors."

"Actually, I believe I owe you one," she said with syrupy sweetness.

He started to reply, but bit off whatever he'd been about to say.

It was just as well. Penny would have hated to pick up the threads of an ancient squabble in front of the two fascinated policemen. She found their obvious respect for Sam, which all the teasing couldn't hide, something of a mystery. She couldn't even figure out how he'd managed to get on the force.

Stories of Sam Roberts's narrow escapes from the law were the stuff of family legend. Her grandfather had tried to regale her with several of them once again just before she'd left L.A., but she'd cut him off. At sixteen, when his sister had married into the Halloran family, Sammy had appeared destined for the life of a con artist at best. Naturally, her grandfather took full credit for his redemption.

But Penny had never gotten the sense that his salvation had been complete enough to land him on the Boston police force. She wondered what the whole story was behind that. She also wondered why no one in California had happened to mention it, then admitted that quite possibly it was because she tended to exit the room whenever his name came up.

Penny glanced over, noted the tension in Sam's stance and the irritation in his expression and wondered if she'd ever get the chance to find out. She told herself it didn't really matter. Sam Roberts clearly wasn't the kind of man who'd be interested in being a pal to some distant relation. He'd made that more than clear years ago. In fact, he looked like the sort of man who viewed women as having one single purpose in life and it sure as heck wasn't friendship.

Of course, that raised the question of why he'd bothered to show up here tonight in the first place. She figured she had her grandfather to thank for that. She wondered what he'd held over Sam's head to get him to agree this time.

Sam's temper had finally cooled sufficiently enough that he could look at Penny Hayden without wanting to murder her. He'd pretty well trampled any little flare-ups of guilt, as well, and was beginning to enjoy watching her trying to extricate herself from any share of the blame for the false alarm.

If she weren't such an obvious pain in the neck, she might be attractive, he thought, idly studying her smooth-as-silk complexion and the dusting of freckles on her turned-up nose.

The kid had gone and grown up on him. She was wearing jeans that fit like a second skin, a denim shirt she'd tied in a knot at her tiny waist and those cowboy boots that she'd used somewhat effectively as weapons. She'd scooped her hair into a ponytail, though most of it had fallen free during their tussle. Sam had the oddest desire to free the rest of it and let it tumble through his fingers. He nixed that notion right away. He had no difficulty whatsoever recognizing trouble and until today he'd gotten fairly adept at sidestepping it. It was a skill he liked to think had come with maturity.

He deliberately forced his glance away and caught Ryan studying him speculatively. "What's your problem?" he growled.

The younger cop grinned. "I'm not the one who came within a hairsbreadth of being hauled in for breaking and entering and assault."

"Oh, go catch some criminals."

"Thought we had," Jake reminded him. "Might even write up a lengthy report on it."

"You do and you'll be hoofing it around the lousiest beat in town come the first blizzard of winter," Sam warned.

"Come on, Jake," Ryan urged, still grinning. "You know what Sam's like when he gets testy. Can't take a joke."

Sam briefly considered pounding their heads together, then decided the subsequent aggravation of explaining why to the heirarchy at headquarters wouldn't be worth it. Fortunately, they seemed ready to beat a hasty retreat.

"Now don't you two go squabbling the minute our backs are turned," Ryan warned cheerfully as he closed the door.

Sam glared after them. As soon as their footsteps faded, Penny whirled on him.

"How could you humiliate me like that?" she demanded.

He regarded her incredulously, remembering with absolute clarity exactly how irritating she could be...and how turned on that tended to make him. Dammit, she could still do it.

"Excuse me?" he said. "If there was any humiliating done around here tonight, it was watching two men I work with come after me with their weapons drawn."

"Served you right. You had no business standing in that hall and scaring me half to death."

He shook his head, refusing to acknowledge the truth in the accusation. "You really are obnoxious."

"Now that's a mature response," she countered. "How can you call me that? It's been years since you even set eyes on me."

"Not nearly long enough," he shot back.

Their gazes clashed, hers every bit as fiery as he knew his must be. He'd stared down hardened criminals more easily. She never even flinched. A little frisson of admiration cut through his irritation. He sighed and let the last of his anger fade away.

"So, Penny Hayden, welcome to Boston."

She didn't seem to be quite so willing to let bygones be bygones. "If you're the kind of welcoming committee this town sends out, I'm surprised anyone ever moves here."

"They usually reserve me for the people they expect might be troublesome. I'd say we're right on track this time."

She rolled her eyes in obvious disgust. "Why are you here, really?"

"At the risk of stirring up a hornet's nest, I'll tell you the God's honest truth."

"A pleasant change," she noted.

Sam shook his head. The woman was constantly spoiling for a fight. At least that was something they had in common. He held on to his patience by a thread. "Granddad Brandon called, said you were just settling in. He wanted me to stop by and see if there was anything I could do to help."

"Was this your idea of help?" she asked. "Couldn't you have called first, warned me you were on your way?"

He shrugged. "Hey, *you* attacked me in that hallway. If you hadn't, I'd have introduced myself politely, just in case you'd forgotten what I looked like, then offered to do anything I could to show you around Boston."

Eyes that were clear and guileless studied him intently. "But you wouldn't have meant it, would you?" she said finally. "Just like last time."

Sam tried to ignore the guilt that cut through him. "Why wouldn't I be happy to show you around?"

"It's a good thing you're on the side of the law," she informed him dryly. "You're a genuinely crummy liar. Remember, I was there the night you dutifully dragged me to a movie. And I know how Granddad can be. It's easier to give in than it is to try to wriggle off his hook. Well, consider your duty done, Sam. I can look out for myself."

To emphasize that she meant what she said, Penny opened the door and waited for him to walk through it. Sam saw no reason not to comply, until he was on the other side, his foot on the top step. Then he realized that he recognized the expression he'd read in her eyes. Not so many years ago, before the Hallorans had come into his life, he'd seen loneliness—and the stubborn determination not to let it show—just by looking in the mirror.

Knowing he was going to regret it, he turned back. "Look, as long as I'm here, why don't we go grab something to eat?"

It wasn't the most gracious invitation he'd ever uttered, but he was offended by the distrust written all over her face. Forcing the words through gritted teeth, he added, "Look, we've gotten off to a bad start here."

"Again," she pointed out, not giving an inch.

He bit off a retaliatory comment and said simply, "I'm sorry."

Her gaze locked on his and his heart took an unexpected leap. He got the distinct feeling he was in over his head and sinking fast.

"I suppose it was partly my fault," she admitted grudgingly. "But dinner's really not necessary."

"Maybe not for you, but I'm starved."

"I meant, it's not necessary that you take me out. We're only distantly related by marriage. It's not like there's some family obligation at stake."

Sam grinned ruefully. "Wanna bet? If I tell Granddad Brandon that I have terrified and deeply offended his precious granddaughter for a second time, he'll call the chief and have me busted back to foot patrol."

Penny regarded him with evident fascination. "Interesting," she declared.

"What?"

"Apparently you spend your life chasing bad guys without fear, but Brandon Halloran terrifies you."

"He doesn't scare you?"

She shook her head. "He's a pussycat."

"Obviously he hasn't gotten around to meddling in your life yet."

"Sure he has," she retorted. "Who do you think sent me to those self-defense classes so I could handle the likes of you?"

Sam chuckled. "Remind me to tell him he wasted his money."

"I'd take a look at my shin and think about the timely arrival of the police before I made cracks like that, if I were you."

"Touché. Now, how about dinner? There's a cute little Italian place just down the street. Rosie makes a ziti with vodka sauce that will bring tears to your eyes."

Penny seemed to be considering the invitation thoughtfully, before finally shrugging. "I suppose it would be worth it, just to see the big, tough policeman cry. Let me grab my purse."

Sam was pleased to see that she did just that. She didn't waste time running off to primp as if this were a date. She just hauled her two-ton purse off the sofa, draped it over her shoulder and followed him from the apartment. He was astounded she didn't walk lopsided.

"What's in that thing?" he asked, trying to peer inside its mysterious depths.

She tugged it away. "A wallet, a brush, makeup, a book, a bottle of mineral water." She shrugged. "You know, the usual necessities."

He shook his head. "Hell, short stuff, next time just take a swing with that thing. It could knock somebody out cold."

"I'll remember that," she said, giving him a look that suggested she still wouldn't mind experimenting with the technique on him.

Sam prided himself on not giving a damn what anyone, except for a handful of family members, thought of him. It worried him that he was beginning to care that Penny Hayden continued to regard him with suspicion even now that she knew who he was. An unfamiliar desire to win her over made him irritable all over again.

Without another word, Sam led the way down the stairs without bothering to check to see if she had any difficulty keeping up with his long stride. If she did, she never complained.

And she was right there beside him when he reached Rosie's, where the bouquet of garlic and tomatoes was more alluring than any expensive French perfume he'd ever encountered. He drew in a deep, satisfying breath and felt some of the tension ease out of him.

"Sammy!" Rosie cried when she spotted him. She enveloped him in an enthusiastic bear hug, then pinched his cheek. "You are too skinny. It has been too long since you have been by to see me. Do I have to be robbed to get you inside my restaurant?"

"I was here two weeks ago," he protested.

"You expect my pasta to sustain you for that long? This is the food of life, *caro*. Pasta and red wine are meant to be eaten every night."

"If I did that, pretty soon I wouldn't be able to haul myself after the criminals. I'd be too fat and lazy."

Rosie waved her hand dismissively. "Always the jokes. I know the truth. You have some other cook you adore. That's it, isn't it?"

"There is no other woman in my life. I swear it," he told her emphatically.

Just then, though, Rosie spotted Penny. "And who is this, then? You pretend that she is not even here, when I can see for myself that she is."

"Rosie, this is Penny Hayden. She has just moved here from Los Angeles. Penny, this is Rosa Di-Martelli, who makes the best pasta this side of Rome."

Rosie's dark eyes scanned Penny from head to toe. A worrisome beam of approval spread across her face. Only one person in Sam's life could match Brandon Halloran when it came to meddling and she was regarding Penny with a very speculative gleam in her eye.

"You live in the neighborhood, yes?" she said to Penny. "I have seen you at the produce stand next door."

"I have an apartment a few blocks away," Penny confirmed.

"Then you will come here often for dinner. That means I will see more of my Sammy."

"Don't go getting any ideas, Rosie," Sam warned.

"What is the fun of life without ideas?" she retorted. "Besides, I can see these same ideas in your eyes."

Sam started to deny it vehemently, but decided to save his breath. An argument would only lend too much weight to Rosie's romantic observations. She grinned as if she'd guessed his thoughts.

"Now, come, sit," she ordered. "I will bring you a bottle of my best wine and I think the ziti with vodka sauce. I will make it special for you, since it is your favorite."

"I could sacrifice and have the lasagna," Sam offered.

"Sacrifice!" She huffed. "Since when is it a struggle to eat any of my food?"

She was still muttering under her breath as she left them to place the order in the kitchen.

"Obviously you're a favorite of hers," Penny noted.

She sounded amazed that anyone could be genuinely fond of him. To his surprise, her astonishment cut. He tried to ignore how much it hurt. He shrugged. "I'm a challenge. She's been trying to fatten me up and marry me off for several years now. The fact that she's still batting zero on both counts makes her crazy."

"I'm surprised you tolerate her interference."

"Wait until you taste her pasta. It's worth any price. Besides, Rosie and I go way back."

"Oh?"

"She helped Dana and I foil the system by playing guardian whenever we needed an adult to keep the social workers at bay."

"You mean, after your mother died?"

Sam nodded. "Dana was determined that the system wasn't going to split us up, even though I was just a kid and she was barely into her teens."

Penny looked fascinated. "Your sister must really be something. I'm looking forward to getting to know her better. We didn't really have nearly enough time together at the christening and I haven't been East since then. Grandfather adores her. He credits Dana with giving him the gumption to go after grandmother one last time when she was resisting all his attempts to get her to marry him."

Sam vividly recalled Brandon's depression during that time. The whole family had been worried sick about him. Dana had taken matters into her own hands.

"She could see how much your grandmother meant to him, even after all the years they were separated," he told Penny. "Once Dana gets an idea in her head, she can move mountains, if that's what it takes. All that determination still scares the dickens out of me. Fortunately, now that she has Jason, plus three kids of her own, plus her sweater design business, she doesn't have much time left to waste on sticking her nose into my business."

Penny sighed with such wistfulness that Sam was taken aback. "What's wrong?"

"I guess I was just wondering what it would have been like to grow up in such a tight-knit family. We hardly ever see my older sisters. Mom and Aunt Kate are pretty close now, but for a while there was a lot of tension between them when they discovered they were only half sisters. I feel like I missed out on so much by not knowing about this extended family on the East Coast until Grandfather came after my grandmother to rekindle their old love affair. Maybe that's why I ended up loving books and science. I could get so absorbed in them, I didn't notice how lonely I was."

"And here I was just thinking that you were the lucky one, growing up with two parents in a house filled with love and stability."

"I guess we never truly appreciate what we have until we see it through other people's eyes."

The surprisingly philosophical and almost friendly conversation died the instant heaping plates of pasta arrived, along with steaming garlic bread and a dry red wine.

"Heaven," Penny murmured a long time later.

Sam pushed away the last of his meal with a similar sigh of contentment. "Coffee?"

"Not another thing," she said. "I should be getting home. I have to be at the lab by seven."

"I thought you were here for grad school."

"I am, but I'm doing a research project, too."

She started to explain it, something about bacteria and virus that sounded pretty lethal to Sam. He was astounded by the glint of excitement in her eyes as she discussed her work. To a man who'd struggled through the bare minimum requirements in high school science, it was an eye-opening experience to discover someone who actually viewed all that stuff with genuine enthusiasm.

"Don't you think there's something a little odd about getting so turned on by a bunch of germs?" he inquired as he walked her back to her apartment.

"You wouldn't feel that way if you had a disease caused by those germs and I had the cure."

He shrugged. "I suppose."

They fell silent after that. Sam glanced down at her and saw an expression that might have been disappointment on her face. That look made him feel guilty all over again. He probably should have feigned an interest in her life's work, but he'd gotten used to being on his own and not doing anything that didn't really appeal to him. Okay, he'd gotten downright selfish.

"Thanks for dinner," she said at her door.

"Sure," he said. He shoved his hands into his pockets and suddenly felt like a kid on a first date with absolutely no idea of what to do next.

"I'm sorry we got off to such a rocky start," he said finally.

"Me, too."

He tried to figure out something else to say, tried to figure out why he had this perfectly ridiculous urge to kiss her until the sadness in her eyes fled. Instead he just backed away, hand lifted in a wave. "See you."

"Yeah, right," she said in a way that told him she didn't believe it any more than he did, but was willing to go along with the polite charade.

Outside, he drew in a deep breath and tried to feel triumphant about having paid off his debt to Granddad Brandon. Instead he felt as if he'd just yanked the wings off a helpless, fragile butterfly.

Chapter Three

Staring into her microscope the following morning, Penny was finally able to put all thoughts of Sam out of her head. It was always like this for her. In the lab, she could retreat to another place, where the only thing that mattered was what she saw magnified on a tiny rectangle of glass. This was a world of mysteries to be unraveled, a world of challenges, a world where she was respected for her mind. It was safe, but never boring.

She took a sip of her coffee, then slipped another slide into place. She was peering intently at the microorganisms and making notes when the phone rang. Impatient at the interruption, she snatched it up.

"Yes?"

"Is that you, Penny, my sweet?"

She sighed and put aside the pen. "Hello, Grandfather." She glanced at her watch. "What are you doing calling at this hour? It's the crack of dawn in California."

"Your grandmother likes to go for a walk before the birds get up. She insists we'll live a lot longer. If you ask me, we're already ahead of the game, but you know how she is. So, how's it going? You settling in okay?"

"I'm doing fine."

"I still think you should have moved into my house. You'd have had it all to yourself most of the time since your grandmother likes the weather better out here."

"I like my apartment. I got to fix it up just the way I wanted to. It's cozy. I'd just be rattling around in that big old place of yours. Besides, you know how I hate to dust."

"That's why I have a housekeeper," he reminded her.

It was a familiar argument, but Penny wasn't inclined to bring it to an end. She knew what would be coming next and it wasn't something she wanted to get into. Before she could think of a way to head him off, he inquired casually, "Has Sam been by yet? He promised he'd drop in on you."

"Oh, he dropped in, all right," she retorted dryly. "Made quite an entrance, in fact."

"What's that mean?"

"It means that of all the idiotic, harebrained schemes you've ever come up with, this one takes the cake. I thought you'd learned your lesson about trying to force Sam and me together nine years ago."

"What scheme? What lesson?" he said, sounding genuinely puzzled.

"You know what I'm talking about. I do not need a baby-sitter. I do not need somebody hanging around me out of pity."

"Oh, fiddle-faddle. Nobody's pitying you, girl."

"Seemed like that to me."

"In case you haven't noticed, which you probably haven't with your head always focused on that microscope or poked into a book, you're a beautiful young woman."

"And you're a biased old man."

He paused at that, then asked quietly, "Okay, then, what about a friend? Couldn't you use one of those? Sam would make a good one."

Penny couldn't imagine the supremely masculine Sam indulging in anything as bland as a casual, platonic friendship with any woman. But maybe men, especially seventy-eight-year-old grandfathers, couldn't recognize such blatant sensuality in another male. She sighed just thinking about the effect the man had on her.

This was no time to dwell on that, though. She had heard the caring and worry in her grandfather's voice. Though he'd never said a word about it, he more than anyone had recognized the bruised feelings Sam had left in his wake after their first encounter. Obviously he'd viewed this manufactured reunion as a chance for Sam to make amends. Little did he know.

"I may be alone, but I'm not lonely," she told him firmly. "But even if I were the loneliest person on earth, I don't think Sam Roberts would be the solution to the problem."

"You two aren't still fussing at each other like a couple of kids in the school yard, are you?"

"Not exactly."

"What exactly?" he persisted.

"I just don't think he and I got off on the right foot for establishing a friendship."

"You mean nine years ago? For goodness' sake, girl, can't you forget about that? That was my fault, more than his. I pushed him because I could see how much it meant to you."

"You're probably right about that," she agreed readily, even though he'd probably hoped she'd let him off the hook.

"I thought you'd be good for each other," he said defensively. "Still do, for that matter."

"You wouldn't feel that way if you'd seen us last night."

This time her grandfather was the one who sighed heavily. "Okay, what went wrong this time?" he asked. He sounded defeated, but she knew better than to believe he'd given up.

Penny described the way she'd mistaken Sam for some maniac. Her grandfather chuckled with unmistakable glee as she told the story. By the time she'd finished, she was able to put aside the odd mix of outrage and embarrassment and laugh with him. "Okay, so in retrospect it was pretty amusing, but I don't think he saw it that way. I humiliated him in front of his colleagues."

"Trust me," Brandon said, "Sam doesn't humiliate too easily. He grew up with a hide like an elephant. He had to."

Penny wasn't so sure. She recalled that tiny spark of dismay in his eyes as his two fellow officers had listened to her scrambling to explain what had happened. Contrary to the image he liked to project, she was beginning to suspect Sam just might be a decent kind of guy. The mistake he'd made years ago had been in trying to please his surrogate grandfather rather than thinking of her feelings. Even that kiss hadn't been a crime. In some ways, the discovery was incredibly disconcerting, fueling the ridiculous attraction she'd always felt and sworn she was over.

She'd probably just imagined that hint of sensitivity, anyway, she told herself sternly. Just as quickly, she countered with the reminder that he had hung out with her the night before. She wasn't sure exactly why he'd insisted on dinner, especially since it had been abundantly clear that he'd have preferred to be almost anywhere else on earth. It was possible that once again he had only done it to please her grandfather. Or maybe he'd intended to satisfy some smidgen of guilt over his own behavior. Less likely, but certainly possible, was that he had recognized her unfamiliar desire for companionship in a new place. At any rate, Sam had been there for her.

"If you're that worried about it, you could call and apologize again," her grandfather said, apparently interpreting her silence as unspoken concern for Sam's feelings. "Send the man some flowers. That'll catch him off guard."

Penny could just imagine the gossip at the police station if a dozen roses turned up on Sam Roberts's desk. The idea held a certain appeal, but she squashed it. She recognized a sneaky tactic when she saw one. Her grandfather was just trying to manipulate another meeting. A dozen roses would leave Sam duty-bound to call.

"When hell freezes over," she muttered. "If anybody apologizes to the man, it ought to be you."

Her grandfather huffed indignantly. Then he said, "Okay, so maybe I will."

Something in his tone warned her she should have let well enough alone.

Penny knew for certain just how big her mistake had been when the phone rang the following day, right when she was in the middle of a critical experiment in the lab.

"Penny, it's Sam."

"Yes," she murmured distractedly, her gaze still locked on what she was seeing through the microscope lens.

"How about dinner?"

That got her attention. "Dinner? You and me? Why? We've done that."

"You have to eat. I have to eat. We might as well do it together," he retorted, his tone losing any last hint of graciousness.

"Granddad," she said with a sigh.

He chuckled at her ready recognition of the source of the invitation. "Okay, he's at it again. I suppose it wouldn't hurt to go along with him for one night, would it?"

"You don't just *go along* with Brandon. The man is capable of steamrolling over the Joint Chiefs of Staff."

"True. But you and I, we're tougher, right?"

Penny hesitated, but she had to admit there was a certain temptation in trying to outwit her grandfather. And she did think of herself as particularly adept at avoiding anything resembling a relationship that might interfere with her work. And despite those little frissons of attraction she'd felt a few days earlier, she was long over her silly infatuation with Sam, wasn't she? So what was the harm?

The wounded look she sometimes saw in Sam Roberts's eyes chose that moment to flicker alive in her memory. The dangerous, sexy smile taunted her. She dismissed them as inconsequential. They were talking about one evening. Dinner. How complicated could it get?

"When?" she said finally.

Her lack of enthusiasm apparently communicated itself to him. "Let's get it over with. Tonight?"

"Fine. What time?"

"I have an appointment at five, but I should be through by six-thirty. If you can meet me there, I know a great restaurant in the neighborhood."

"Is it half as good as Rosie's?"

"Maybe even better, but don't ever tell her I said that."

"Hmm," she said thoughtfully. "Something to hold over your head. I like that."

"Watch it, short stuff," he warned, but he was chuckling when he gave her the address. "See you later."

Penny started to remind him to stop calling her "short stuff," then realized that every time he used the affectionate phrase she automatically recalled how much larger and more powerfully built he was. It was downright interesting the way her thoughts always came back to settle on an image of how blasted attractive the man was. He probably did it intentionally for just that reason.

"Later," she agreed, and wished her pulse wasn't suddenly racing in anticipation.

Sam changed into his boxing shorts in the locker room, then went through the gym in search of Johnny, who'd owned the place forever. He found him in his cramped, paper-strewn office. He picked a box of invoices up off of the room's only spare chair and plopped them on the floor.

"Are you ever going to clean this place?" he inquired, grinning at the grizzled old man who owned this seedy old barn of a gym.

Johnny's Place made up in atmosphere what it lacked in high-tech exercise equipment. This was the kind of gym that world heavyweight champs would feel comfortable in. Some had even trained here in preparation for title bouts a few decades back, according to local legend. And Johnny had yellowing, dog-eared, autographed photos of some of the best on the walls of his cluttered office. Right now, as always, he looked horrified by Sam's suggestion that he straighten up.

"And mess up my filing system?" he protested. "Why would I want to go and do that after all these years?"

"You might discover you're rich."

"Or that I'm close to bankruptcy. Either way, it's better not to know. As long as I've got enough for dinner and some bottles of linament, I figure business is good."

"Has Randy been coming around to help out?" Sam asked, referring to the seventeen-year-old he was supposed to box in a few minutes. He'd brought the teen here to work out his frustrations, much as Jason had brought Sam years earlier.

"He shows up pretty regular," Johnny said evasively.

"How regular is that?"

"Every couple of days. Sticks around for a few hours. I don't have that much for him to do."

"I thought he was going to help with this paperwork. He has a good head on his shoulders and math was the one subject he passed with flying colors."

"He tries, but like I said, things are a little disorganized in here."

Sam sensed that Johnny was holding something back. He wasn't entirely sure he wanted to know what, but he'd gotten Johnny into this. He owed it to him to see that nothing went wrong. "What aren't you telling me?" he asked.

The aging boxer regarded him with regret. "Hey, I don't want to go telling tales."

"Come on, Johnny. What's going on?"

"The kid's got these friends, okay?" He shuddered. "I gotta tell you, Sammy, they give me the creeps. I don't want 'em hanging around."

Sam could see how much Johnny hated making the admission. And coming from an old boxer who wasn't afraid of much, the fear had to be taken seriously. Besides, Sam knew exactly which friends Johnny was talking about. They were precisely the reason he'd gotten Randy the job at the gym. He sighed.

"I don't blame you," he told Johnny. "Thanks for trying. I'll talk to Randy, but if he doesn't want to make the break from this gang of his, I'll try to figure out something else."

Johnny regarded him worriedly. "I hope to hell he'll listen. He's a good kid. I can see that. But those friends of his are real trouble."

Back in the gym, Sam pulled on his gloves and started warming up at one of the punching bags. Randy, trailed by the two-bit criminals he considered his pals, finally showed at five-fifteen. All of them were wearing black jeans and black T-shirts with the logo of some rap group that thrived on violent lyrics. They all had haircuts that could break a mother's heart. Most of them had diamond studs in one ear. Probably real, Sam thought, wondering which jeweler they'd ripped off.

He shot a disapproving frown at Randy. "You're late."

"Sorry. We were tied up."

Sam could just imagine what had detained them. They'd probably been staking out a business to rob. He bit back a suggestion that Randy send his delinquent buddies on their way. Maybe he could do something to get through to all of them. Okay, so he suffered from delusions, but it was worth a shot.

"Any of you guys want to go a few rounds?" he inquired.

"Nah. We're just fixing to watch Ran-dall," Tank Landry informed him. The scrawny, dark-haired kid with mean eyes already had an impressive rap sheet for someone not even out of his teens. All pretty tame stuff so far, but it was only a short leap from burglary to armed robbery.

Sam read the anticipation on Tank's face. He was probably hoping Randy would pound the cop into the ropes. Fortunately, Randy wasn't that quick on his feet yet. With a little practice, though, Tank and his associates could get their wish. Tonight, however, maybe it would do them some good to see that one of their own wasn't nearly as tough as they imagined.

Before they entered the ring, he pulled Randy aside and nodded toward the onlookers. "I thought we had a deal."

Randy cast an uneasy glance in their direction. "Shaking loose ain't as easy as I thought."

"Do you want the job here or not? If you don't, I've got kids lined up who'd jump at it."

Randy regarded him with dismay. "Come on, man. You can't do that. You told me Johnny needs somebody who can do math like me to help with that mess in his office."

"I'm sure some of them can add and subtract, too. I'll find out which ones can, if you don't keep these jerks out of this place and out of your life." Sam used his glove to tilt Randy's chin up so he could look into his eyes as he warned, "They'll drag you down with them if they can, Randy."

The boy looked miserable and frightened. Sam could understand how he felt. If Randy made the break, he'd lose the only friends he'd ever known. A series of foster homes hadn't given him much in the way of family. Tank's gang was all he had. They might even retaliate for his defection. It took courage to face that.

Months ago, when he'd busted Randy for petty theft, Sam had seen something of himself in the troubled teen. He'd wanted desperately to steer him onto the right path before it was too late. Saving a kid like Randy was the whole reason he'd joined the police force, rather than taking the nice, cushy job in sales at Halloran Industries that had been waiting for him. Brandon had been saddened by his choice, but he'd supported him in it.

"Well, what's it going to be?" Sam asked, refusing to relent.

"I'll tell 'em to get lost," Randy promised. "Just let me do it in my own way."

Sam nodded. "Fair enough, but do it soon. I mean it."

He figured that victory meant a lot more than the one that followed in the ring.

"Nice job. You landed some great punches," he told Randy when they climbed out of the ring. "You're developing a nice left hook. I'm going to have to start watching myself."

The teen struggled against a grin and lost. "Johnny's been working with me," he admitted. Suddenly his gaze seemed to be riveted on something just beyond Sam. He gave a slow, approving whistle. "How come we don't get more regulars down here who look like that?"

Even without turning around, Sam guessed he was referring to Penny. He also had the oddest desire to level the kid with a punch to his jaw. He glanced over his shoulder and caught Penny staring at him in openmouthed shock. If he hadn't been so irritated by Randy's blatant reaction to her, he might have been amused by the expression on her face. She looked as if she'd never seen a sweaty, bare-chested man before in her life.

Suddenly feeling surprisingly territorial, he left Randy without a word and strolled over to her. "I have a few rounds left in me. Care to hop in the ring?"

Her mouth snapped shut. She still couldn't seem to take her eyes off of him, though. Finally she said in a faintly horrified whisper, "You've been brawling."

"Boxing," he corrected.

"What's the difference?"

"In the ring we fight by the rules."

"Rules?" she repeated in a choked voice. "What kind of rules give a grown man permission to beat up on that poor kid? He has blood on his face."

"Split lip," Sam acknowledged. "He has to learn to duck."

"You . . . you . . ."

For the first time since he'd met her, she seemed to be at a loss for words. "Savage," he supplied cheerfully. He'd heard most of the arguments against boxing before.

She blinked at his ready admission. "Yes, that's it. Savage. How can you do that?"

He shrugged. "I learned from one of the best. He suggested it was an improvement over brawling in alleys."

Penny was clearly unimpressed. "Sounds like the sort of argument you'd get from that disreputable-looking man I saw in the office on my way in."

"Actually, it was Jason who brought me here."

Her eyes widened in obvious disbelief. "Jason Halloran?"

"The very one. He boxed in college. So did his father. And even Brandon enjoyed going a few rounds."

"I don't believe it."

"Ask them. Actually it's good exercise. Dana comes down here with Jason every once in a while. She can slam a punching bag with the best of them. She says it's better than slugging one of the kids."

"I suppose," Penny said doubtfully.

Sam grinned at her. "Personally, I think she likes to look at all the bare-chested guys."

Penny's gaze drifted back to the bare chest smack in front of her. She swallowed hard and cleared her throat. "Um, yes, I suppose I can understand the fascination."

Sam chuckled. "Anytime you're through, I'll go shower and change."

She blinked and looked at him in confusion. "What?"

He gestured toward the locker room. "A shower."

Still looking shaken, she nodded. "I'll wait outside."

"No, you won't. This isn't the best area for a lady to be hanging around on the street alone. Wait in Johnny's office. He won't mind. I cleared off a chair earlier, so I know there's a place to sit."

She nodded and, still looking somewhat dazed, wandered off in the direction of the office. It took Sam slightly longer to move. Penny's innocent fascination with his body had had an incredibly arousing effect on him. The reaction both stunned and worried him. The last thing he needed was to be affected in any way whatsoever by Penny Hayden.

"Well, well, well," Tank Landry said, following Penny's departure with a leering expression. "Looks like the cop has a lady friend. I'll bet she'd rather get to know a real man."

Sam glared at him, but he managed to keep his voice calm. "You get within one mile of the lady and you'll answer to me, smart guy."

A calculating gleam lit Tank's black eyes. "It's always good to know what your enemies really prize. You just made a big mistake, *smart guy.*"

It took every last bit of control Sam possessed to keep from slamming his glove into the punk's midsection, then following that by a punch straight to his smug face. He knew, though, that he had made a terrible miscalculation by warning Tank away from Penny. He had inadvertently made her a target for this gang of street toughs. They loved nothing more than taking away what belonged to someone else, be it a television set, a car, or a woman.

The possibility of this creep laying one finger on Penny sickened Sam. Like it or not, he was going to be keeping a very close eye on her, at least until he felt relatively certain that Tank and his buddies had lost interest.

He realized with dismay that the prospect of sticking close to her worried him almost as much as what might happen if he didn't.

Chapter Four

Dinner had been a bad idea. Sam wondered why he hadn't left well enough alone after their disastrous meeting a few nights earlier. Oh, sure, some of the decision to ask Penny out had been in response to Brandon Halloran's latest round of needling, but the real bottom line was that he hadn't been able to get her out of his mind.

To his astonishment and deep regret, she'd gotten under his skin with those big blue eyes, which communicated whatever emotion she was feeling—hurt, anger, loneliness, and something that might have been adoration. Hurt, anger and loneliness were things Sam knew a lot about, emotions with which he could empathize.

As for adoration, if that's what it had been, well, she'd get over that quickly enough. He told himself it was nothing to panic about, no reason to avoid her as if she had some contagious disease. He'd had lots of practice at keeping women at arm's length. Most of them made the decision to go on their own, once they'd realized that even physical intimacy would not lead to a full-fledged relationship, much less marriage.

In Penny's case, discouragement should be even easier, he decided midway through dinner. All he would need to do would be to bring up his work as an undercover cop. She seemed about as impressed with that as she had been with the gym. In fact, she looked downright horrified as he talked about the increase in gang-related violence and the sad, dysfunctional kids who had nowhere else to turn for acceptance. For some reason he couldn't explain, he was oddly disappointed by her reaction.

"Like those boys at the gym?" she asked, her distaste evident. "The ones who looked as if they were about to pull guns and shoot up the place? You honestly think they can be salvaged? I thought the police force was the last place I'd find some bleeding heart liberal. Grandfather would have a stroke if he knew what you were up to."

Sam shook his head. "I don't think so. In fact, he's the main reason I became a policeman."

She regarded him with obvious disbelief. "You can't mean that."

"Oh, but I do. When I met the Hallorans, I was a lot like those boys you saw at the gym, just itching to get into trouble, searching for a way to feel important. Dana was worried sick about me. Jason wanted to turn me around for her sake, but let's just say he found my immediate response discouraging. Brandon, however, actually saw something good in me and set out to teach me some self-esteem. I figure his faith saved me. I owe it to him to do whatever I can for some other kid who's headed down a dangerous path."

"And you honestly don't think those boys are beyond redemption?"

"Not all of them," he said cautiously.

Penny regarded him so intently that he found himself warming under the scrutiny. The reaction was particularly disturbing since there was nothing the least bit intimate in her perusal. If anything, she merely looked worried, as if she were concerned about his safety. His body, however, seemed to be responding as if she were visually stripping him naked. These wayward thoughts were beginning to get irksome, especially when he'd made a firm decision to play it cool around Penny so that she didn't misunderstand his intentions and get hurt a second time.

"The one whose lip you split, he's the one you think has a chance, isn't he?" she said finally.

Sam nodded, glad to have something to talk about to get his mind off his unexpectedly rampaging hormones. "He's had a lot of bad breaks," he explained, trying to find a way to make her understand why Randy's future had become so important to him. "He's been in some lousy foster homes. All he wants is someplace to belong, somebody to care. Up until now his only choice has been that gang of thugs you saw with him today."

Penny shuddered. "Quite an adoptive family."

Sam debated whether to tell her that those charming young men had their eyes on her. Unless he planned to keep her under twenty-four-hour surveillance, he had to. She needed to be more alert to her surroundings, to replace her instinctively trusting nature with some realistic cynicism.

"There's something you ought to know," he said finally.

She paused with a forkful of pasta halfway to her mouth. "I don't think I like the way you said that."

"You're psychic now?"

"No, but I'm beginning to recognize that somber, protective look. Grandfather gets it all the time. It's some Halloran family trait."

"I'm not a Halloran," he reminded her irritably.

"Close enough. Come on, spill it. What's the bad news?"

"Tank . . ."

"The boy with the split lip?" she inquired almost hopefully.

"No, the one who looks as if he enjoys torture."

"A pleasant description."

"Unfortunately, an accurate one."

"Okay, what about him?"

"He's gotten the notion that I...that you and I..." He fumbled for a description that wouldn't stir up a hornet's nest. Unfortunately, there wasn't one.

"Are an item?" she supplied helpfully.

There was a definite twinkle in her eyes. For some inexplicable reason he found her amusement irritating. "Right."

"Big deal. Tank's thought process and opinions rank right up there with some national tabloid's. I don't think we ought to worry about them."

"Wrong," Sam said succinctly. "In this case, they're very important."

"Why?"

"Because he and I aren't on the best of terms. I've busted him a few times. He might try to get to me through you."

Penny swallowed hard. Every trace of amusement vanished. "Does that mean what I think it does?"

"It means I don't want you taking any stupid, unnecessary chances."

She regarded him with something that might have been weary resignation. "You mean, like ever leaving my apartment again, don't you?"

Sam grinned at her perceptiveness. "That's certainly the one I like the best."

"But it's not very practical, is it? Come on, you don't really think he'd come near me, do you? If anything happened to me, he'd be the first person you'd suspect."

"Remember what you were saying about Tank's thought process? I don't think he's dealing with an entirely full deck when it comes to logic. Right now, he's going with his gut instinct and that tells him that hurting you will hurt me."

"Well, he's wrong," Penny said, attempting to sound blasé and failing. "Didn't you tell him that? You don't give a hoot about me."

"That's not entirely true," Sam said cautiously, sensing that he was tiptoeing through a mine field. How could he explain that no one was more surprised than he was to discover that he was attracted to her and in the same breath announce that it didn't mean a damn thing? Talk about mixed signals. This was the stuff that could put a woman in therapy for years, or so he'd been told by a few of his past victims.

Penny was watching him with a puzzled expression. "I think maybe you'd better explain," she said, though she didn't sound as if she really wanted to hear an answer.

He sorted through a variety of explanations until he came up with one that sounded sufficiently vague. "Tank might have picked up on some vibes I was sending out."

"What vibes?"

"The usual macho stuff," he replied.

He could read the precise instant when understanding dawned. Pink flooded into her cheeks. It might have been embarrassment, but he had a hunch it was outrage.

"Let me get this straight," she said slowly.

He winced at her tone. He was right. She was furious. As if to prove it, she glared at him. He could imagine the withering effect it would have on most men. For some reason, it excited him. Talk about inappropriate responses. She'd probably belt him, if she guessed. He tried to focus on what she was saying.

"You were acting all possessive and probably making a crude comment or two about your woman," she began, keeping her eyes pinned on him for a reaction. "And he, quite naturally I might add, took this hands-off attitude to mean that I was your personal property. Am I getting close?"

"Close enough," he conceded.

"And now, thanks to you, that thug wants to tattoo my name on his chest?" she snapped facetiously.

Sam thought she was taking it rather well, all things considered. She was mad, not terrified. "That's one of the things he could have on his mind," he agreed. "I'd say there are others you should be more concerned about."

"What should be at the top of the list? Kidnapping? Rape? Murder?"

"I don't think he'll go that far," Sam said defensively.

"But you don't know that, do you?"

"Penny, I'm going to protect you."

"Oh, right," she said with heavy sarcasm. "You're the one who got me into this. You and Grandfather. Remind me to thank him, too."

"You're not going to tell him?" Sam couldn't keep the horrified note out of his voice. He could just imagine the repercussions of that. He'd get a call from the chief the next morning assigning him as Penny's personal bodyguard...probably without pay. He figured it would take less than a week of twenty-four-hour-a-day duty to drive him absolutely over the edge. The maddening desire he had to kiss her would probably flourish into a yearning for a whole lot more.

"Give me one reason I shouldn't tell him," she retorted.

"I'll wind up sleeping on your sofa, sharing your bathroom, following you to work, sitting in a corner of the lab while you do whatever you do. Are you getting the picture?"

"Oh, God," she said.

She said it with a soft little moan that did astonishing things to his insides. She looked as if she were ready to weep. To forestall that, he asked hurriedly, "Does that mean you'll keep this just between us?"

"I suppose I don't have any choice."

She sounded so totally despondent that Sam wanted to hug her. Hugging was not something that came naturally. "That doesn't mean I don't intend to keep an eye on you," he said. Even to his own ears, it sounded grudging. "I do feel responsible for this and I'll handle it in my own way."

"What way is that?" she inquired.

Since neither of them had touched a bite in the past twenty minutes, he figured dinner was a total loss. He waved for the check. "Don't worry," he told her, "I'm still working on it."

She rolled her eyes. "I can hardly wait."

He stood. "Come on. Obviously we've both lost our appetite. I'll take you home."

She sat right where she was, a stubborn expression on her face. "Not necessary. I can catch a cab from here."

Sam felt his stomach clench. Saints protect him from mule-headed, foolhardy women, especially this one. Hadn' she heard one word of what he'd been telling her about Tank's intentions?

"I will take you home," he insisted. "If you want to get yourself killed, do it on somebody else's watch."

She grinned at him. It looked forced.

"What a charming way to put it," she commented.

There was no mistaking the sarcasm in her voice. Sam figured it was a good thing she'd agreed to keep her grandfather out of this. Enforced proximity for the two of them would be more dangerous than anything Tank could devise. Sam had a hunch he would end up strangling the mouthy woman himself.

Sam had seemed extraordinarily unwilling to leave her apartment once he'd safely deposited her there, Penny thought as she toweled her hair dry. Under other circumstances, she might have felt flattered, maybe even experienced a little thrill of anticipation at all that attention. As it was, she figured he'd merely been acting on this insane obligation he felt he had to play bodyguard.

But she had sent him packing. She had even watched out of her window to make sure that he'd actually climbed back into his car, started the engine and driven off. Of course, for all she knew he was parked around the corner, but at least he wasn't in her direct line of sight.

Of all the humiliating moments in her life, one of the worst had to be discovering that Sam had allowed some streetwise punk to believe that he and she...that they were...

She couldn't even bear to think about it, especially when the reality couldn't be further from the dirty little innuendos.

Oh, who was she trying to kid? What really ticked her off was that, despite everything that had happened, some genuinely mentally disturbed part of her wanted those innuendos to be true. Sam made her tingle deep inside. Always had. Apparently always would.

Of course, he also made her furious deep inside. Maybe there was a correlation she ought to examine more closely before she ascribed those sensations to lust rather than a particularly violent form of outrage.

While she was trying to give that possibility some rational, objective consideration, the phone rang. Given the hour, she figured it had to be her grandfather or her mother. She debated the wisdom of talking to either one of them considering her present state of mind and allowed her answering machine to pick up.

She immediately recognized Sam's voice and the edge-of-panic tone as he shouted her name.

"Penny, where the hell are you? Dammit, you'd better not have gone back out again."

She sighed heavily and picked up the receiver. "I'm here," she said. "Are you aware that it is nearly midnight?"

"You weren't asleep."

He said it in a way that sounded more like a comment than a question.

"How would you know that?" she demanded.

"Your lights were still on."

That tingling started up again. "Where are you?" she inquired suspiciously, creeping closer to the window to peer outside.

"In my car."

She groaned. "Where?"

"On my way home. I just happened to drive past and saw the lights."

And pigs fly, she thought.

"I just wanted to check and make sure everything was okay," he said. His voice trailed off as if even he recognized how weak the explanation sounded.

"Did it ever occur to you that I might sleep with the lights on?" she asked.

"That's something people do when they're scared. Nothing's happened since I dropped you off, has it?"

She restrained the urge to laugh hysterically. "It wasn't enough that you warned me that my name is high on a list to become a crime victim?"

"I'm sorry," he said softly.

Penny had to admit he sounded genuinely regretful. "I'll survive."

"I didn't mean to frighten you. I just wanted you to be on your guard."

"Isn't that the same thing?"

"Yeah, I suppose it is. I'm sorry. I could hang around outside if that'll help you get to sleep."

Penny suddenly felt the strongest yearning to have him do just that, just so he'd be close, but she couldn't. Not under false pretenses.

"I'll be fine," she told him. "Go on home and get some sleep."

"Are you sure? It's no trouble. I pull a lot of all-nighters in this car when I'm working a case."

"There's no need to on my account," she assured him.

"Okay. If you say so."

"I do."

"Good night, then."

"Sam?"

"Yes?"

"I wasn't scared."

"If you say so, short stuff," he said.

Penny could practically see the smile tugging at his lips. "I wasn't," she repeated adamantly. "I'd just gotten out of the shower. I never go to bed much before one."

He chuckled aloud at that. "You enjoyed that, didn't you?"

"What?" she inquired innocently.

"Taunting me?"

"Now that you mention it, yes. I enjoyed it quite a bit. 'Night, Sam."

"I'll get even, short stuff. That's a promise."

There was that tingling again, Penny thought, smiling as she hung up the phone. This time she knew *exactly* what it meant. Forget Tank. Sam was the man who was downright dangerous.

Chapter Five

"Are you aware that there's a man following you?" Didi Rogers asked Penny a week later as they walked from the lab to a nearby restaurant for lunch.

Penny whirled around, half expecting to see Tank Landry trailing along behind them. It wouldn't have been the first time. She had spotted him on two different occasions after Sam had warned her to be on the lookout. Both times Randy had been with him, watching worriedly, looking as if he were ready to intercede if Tank made a move on her. So far, though, he had never actually approached her. Just his presence, which confirmed Sam's warning, had unnerved her badly enough. She'd been determined, however, not to let him disrupt her life.

Now, however, the man she spotted about half a
block back was Sam himself. He wasn't doing much
to hide his presence, unless he considered those mir-
rored aviator sunglasses as sufficient disguise. Penny
wondered how Didi had happened to notice him.
Foolish question. Didi noticed any man over the age
of consent. Her radar would detect a male as gorgeous as Sam if he was within a radius of miles. That
didn't explain why she had assumed he was following Penny.

"What makes you think anyone is following me?"
she asked the pathologist who'd provided her with
invaluable assistance in the lab, as well as a lot of
lighthearted moments over the past couple of weeks.
Other than her work, there was very little else that
Didi took seriously. She had an optimistic, slightly
skewed view of life that echoed the outlook Penny
had once had in what seemed another lifetime.

"Because I've seen the man every single day for a
solid week now," she informed Penny.

"So what?" Penny countered. "This area is
crawling with people who take the same route every
day."

"But this person waits outside the lab at noon. He
turns up just outside wherever we happen to go for
lunch. And he's back at the lab when we get off. Since
I don't know him, I figure you must. I'm trained to
look for patterns and draw conclusions, remember?"

Penny grinned ruefully. "I could have sworn your
specialty was DNA, though."

Didi shrugged dramatically. "What can I tell you? Sometimes the habit carries over into other parts of my life. When an experiment goes really badly, I consider changing professions and becoming a P.I. Today's one of those days." She studied Penny closely. "You don't seem to be particularly shocked, or terrified, or indignant. What's the story? Are you on friendly terms with this hunk?"

"Actually, he's distantly related by marriage."

Didi looked skeptical. "So distantly related that he's not allowed to actually speak to you?"

Penny sighed, glad to be at the restaurant where the noise level was so high that any real conversation was virtually impossible. "It's a long story," was all she said, hoping that would end it. Naturally it didn't. Didi had the tenacity of a pit bull once something fascinated her. Obviously a man like Sam would.

"That's the best kind," she said, forcing Penny into the most private booth available in the crowded restaurant. "Tell me everything," she shouted over the noise.

When Penny remained stubbornly silent, burying herself behind the menu she already knew by heart, Didi started to slide out of the booth.

"Where are you going?" Penny asked with a sinking sensation in the pit of her stomach.

"If you won't talk, maybe he will. I'm going to ask him to join us."

"Don't you dare." It came out as more plea than order.

Didi's eyes widened with evident fascination. "It gets more interesting by the minute. I'm waiting. And you might as well put down that menu. You always order the same thing, soup and half a tuna salad sandwich on white toast. You're incredibly boring, Hayden. Or at least you have been up until now. That man outside indicates you might have promise."

"I was not put on this earth to fill your insatiable appetite for amusement," Penny reminded her.

"Perhaps not, but for the next thirty minutes, you're all I've got. Start talking."

Giving in to the inevitable, Penny gave her the short version of her history with Sam and the reason for his presence outside.

Didi looked more and more intrigued. "I think that's sweet," she finally pronounced.

"What? That he made me a target for a gang of hoodlums?"

"No, of course not. I think it's sweet that he's looking out for you." She peered out the window. "He must get awfully tired of just standing around out there. I'm going to invite him to join us for dessert."

She slipped out of the booth and disappeared before Penny could mutter a vehement protest, much less remind her that neither of them ever ate dessert. Suddenly, however, she was stuck with a powerful yearning for something decadent, chocolate, and at least three thousand calories. Maybe that would get her mind off the man who was about to join them.

It didn't surprise her that Didi came back with Sam in tow. She'd never met anyone who could stand up to her. Most men, enchanted by her bubbling personality and long, shapely legs, didn't even want to. Though she was nearing forty, Didi admitted to no more than thirty-five and she had a string of suitors that a college homecoming queen would envy. Sam seemed faintly bewildered at having been reeled in. Penny almost felt sorry for him.

"I understand you're becoming a familiar figure on campus," Penny told him dryly. "I hope you're more discreet at the rest of your undercover work."

"Actually, you're something of a special case."

"You probably want this Tank person to know you're always watching," Didi guessed.

Sam regarded her as if she'd just given the correct answer for the twenty-five-thousand-dollar top prize on a game show. Penny felt vaguely disgruntled by their almost instantaneous rapport. Sam never looked at her like that. He generally looked as if he wanted to throttle her.

"Don't you have some official police business you should be doing?" Penny inquired.

"Actually my current case and this special surveillance have dovetailed rather nicely," he informed her cheerfully.

"All roads lead back to Tank, so to speak."

"Exactly," he said.

He said it so distractedly that Penny wondered exactly where under the table Didi's hand had wandered. She glowered at the pair of them. She knew one sure way to get Sam's attention. "How'd he slip away from you yesterday?" she asked sweetly.

Sam's head snapped around at that. "What are you talking about?"

"I had dinner at Rosie's last night. Tank was outside when I left."

Sam's jaw clenched. "Did he come anywhere near you?"

"If he had, do you think I would be sitting here calmly? I'd probably be skewering you with a fork for getting me into this mess."

"Why didn't you call me?"

"I didn't need you."

"You could have. You should never have left that restaurant alone." He smacked his fist on the table in obvious exasperation. "Damm it, Penny, when will you get it through your head that this isn't a game?"

Their gazes clashed.

"And when will you get it through your thick skull that I am not some five-year-old who needs somebody to baby-sit her?" she shot right back.

"Maybe when you stop acting like one," he countered irritably.

"My, my, my," Didi murmured. "This is better than 'The Young and the Restless.'"

"Who asked you?" Penny muttered.

"I guess I'm going to have to call in reinforcements," he told her, his expression resigned.

"Should I be on the lookout for Jake and Ryan? I'm sure they'd love to hear about this new wrinkle in our family feud." She enjoyed the dull red that crept into his face at the mention of his police colleagues.

"I was thinking of Jason."

So much for the upper hand, she thought dismally. She regarded him with genuine dismay. "Oh, no. Leave Jason out of this. It's only one short leap from him to Grandfather."

"It is, isn't it?" Sam agreed, suddenly looking rather pleased with himself.

"I thought we agreed that Grandfather shouldn't know anything about this."

"Keeping him in the dark did seem like a good idea at the time," Sam said thoughtfully. "Now I'm not so sure."

"Well, I am."

"If you won't cooperate..." He allowed the threat to trail off.

"What is it that you want from me?"

"I could answer that," Didi muttered.

Penny stomped on her foot under the table. At least she thought it was Didi's until she caught the amusement in Sam's eyes. He actually looked triumphant. She gave him a moment to gloat.

"I want you to call me directly or at the very least 9-1-1 the minute you see Tank lurking around again," he ordered.

"And what should I tell 9-1-1?" she inquired sweetly. "Should I mention that Detective Sam Roberts irritated a thug and said thug plans to take it out on me?"

He scowled at her. "Just tell 'em there's a suspicious person stalking you. We have a very good stalking law on the books. Since you have a credible witness to his threat, namely me, we should be able to get a restraining order."

"Don't you think that could get complicated?"

Sam turned to Didi. "Would you please tell this woman to keep her irritation with me from interfering with her common sense."

Didi's eyebrows lifted a fraction. "Sounds to me like you just told her yourself."

"But she doesn't listen to me."

Penny stood. "Maybe that's because you talk to me or around me as if I don't have a brain in my head. Just for the record, Roberts, I did not leave that restaurant alone last night. The instant I saw Tank outside, I had Rosie's boyfriend escort me home. I'm sure you've met Maynard. He won the Mr. Universe contest a few decades back and he's never let those muscles go to seed."

"Why the hell didn't you say so?" he asked, clearly exasperated.

She smiled at him. "You never asked."

With that final shot fired, she took off. She was almost back at the lab when Didi caught up with her.

"Why'd you go running off like that?"

Penny regarded her as if she were running seriously short on logic. "Do you really need to ask?"

"He's genuinely worried about you, you know."

"He's only worried that something will happen to me and the whole family will blame him."

Didi shook her head. "That's not the way I read it. There was enough electricity sparking between the two of you to replace the annual Fourth of July fireworks extravaganza over Boston Harbor."

"Sorry. What you felt were the reverberations of two previously immovable objects slamming together. A force of nature, nothing more."

Didi grinned. "A force of nature, huh? I suppose that's one name for it. Where I come from we call it love."

A force of nature. *Love?* Please! Didi couldn't have been more wrong. Antipathy, maybe. Penny could believe that. She and Sam seemed to have settled into a comfortable routine of hostility. They brought out the very worst in each other, automatically, every single time.

Penny sighed. It really was too bad that all that sizzle couldn't be turned in another direction, but she wasn't going to hold her breath. Besides, how would she survive a relationship with a man who spent his time hanging out with hoodlums, putting his life on the line for punks who didn't appreciate it?

She'd just made a firm decision to avoid involvement when someone tapped rather imperiously on her front door. The only person she knew in Boston who acted as if a closed door was tantamount to an insult was Sam. What on earth would he be doing dropping by unannounced, unless he wanted to pick up his lecture where he'd left off at lunch? Well, she was more than willing to go another round or two. In fact, she found the prospect downright exhilarating.

"I'm coming," she shouted back, snatching papers and books off of every surface she passed and stacking them together in a relatively neat pile on the coffee table. There was no need for the man to discover that housekeeping ranked somewhere below boxing on her list of priorities.

Apparently her belated attempt to tidy up took too long. The knocking resumed, this time with even more force. She flung open the door to find not Sam but her grandparents in the hallway.

"What are you doing here?" she asked, regarding them with astonishment. Only after the words were out of her mouth did she realize how inhospitable she sounded. Judging from her grandmother's suddenly uncertain expression, she at least hadn't mistaken the lack of welcome. Brandon was less easily offended.

"I'm sorry," she apologized in a rush. "It's just that you caught me off guard. Come in." She hugged her grandmother and stood on tiptoe to kiss her grandfather's cheek.

"Brandon, I told you we should have called first," her grandmother said. "Penny probably has plans for the evening."

He waved his hand in a dismissive gesture. "Oh, fiddle-faddle, she can always throw us out, if she needs to leave." He regarded her hopefully. "You got a date?"

"No."

"Oh," he said, clearly disappointed. "Thought maybe you and Sam might have plans."

"Now why would you think a thing like that?"

Her grandmother shot a warning look at her grandfather. For once, thankfully, he took the hint and dropped the matter.

"So, this is your apartment," he said, pacing around the tiny living room. "Not much space."

"I think it's charming," her grandmother said hurriedly. "You've fixed it up beautifully. I love all the plants in the windows."

Her grandfather scowled. "Didn't say she hadn't. I just hate to think of her all cramped up."

"I love it," she reassured him. "It's cozy. Can I get you something? A drink? Coffee? Tea?"

"Tea would be nice," her grandmother said. "Then we'd like to take you out to dinner."

Penny had the oddest feeling that dinner would be a very bad idea. Her grandparents clearly had something on their minds and she had a hunch she didn't want to know what it was. "Actually, I'm afraid I can't join you." She gestured toward the hastily stacked papers and books on the coffee table. "I'm working on a paper for class."

"Nonsense," her grandfather said. "You have to eat. It won't be a late evening. After our trip we don't want to be out so late ourselves."

They followed her as she went into the kitchen, lingering in the doorway when they realized there wasn't room for all of them in the cramped space. She put the teakettle on. "You still haven't said what you're doing here. You didn't mention any plans to come to Boston the last time I talked to you."

"You know your grandfather," her grandmother said, gazing at him with amused affection. "He was getting restless."

Feeling left out was more like it, Penny thought. He probably figured things were going on in Boston that he ought to be controlling and manipulating. Things like her relationship with Sam.

"I was *not* restless," her grandfather countered. "My first great-grandbaby's birthday is this coming weekend. Do you think I wanted to miss the celebration?"

"That's right," Penny said. She looked at her grandmother. "Elizabeth Lacey's going to be ten, right?" She grinned, recalling the stories of how that birth had disrupted her grandparents' wedding reception. "And you two are celebrating a tenth anniversary. Any big parties planned?"

"That's why we stopped by, actually," her grandmother said. "Besides taking you out to dinner, I mean. We wanted to invite you to come out to the Cape. Kevin and Lacey are inviting the whole family out for the weekend. They'd really like you to come. They said they haven't seen hide nor hair of you since you've been in Boston."

"I know," Penny said, thinking of her mother's half brother and his wife, whom she'd barely gotten to know all those years ago at the christening and hadn't seen since. "I've been meaning to call, but getting settled has taken every spare minute I've had.

I have talked to Dana a few times, but our schedules are so hectic we haven't been able to get together.''

Her grandfather snorted disparagingly. "How long could it take to settle into a place this size?"

"Brandon!" Her grandmother frowned at him.

"Oh, hell, Lizzy, I just think she ought to be someplace where there's room enough to turn around. A man feels like he's suffocating in a space this size."

Penny grinned at him. "Then it's a good thing no man is spending much time here, isn't it?"

Her grandfather scowled at her. "Is that a hint?"

"Take it however you like."

"Okay, okay," he grumbled. "We'll get out of your hair, as long as you promise to come out to the Cape on Friday."

"I don't have a car," she reminded him before she considered what the consequences of that remark might be. She could just envision Sam once more being drafted into duty.

"Then we'll pick you up at the lab," her grandmother offered hurriedly just as her grandfather started to open his mouth. He glared at his wife.

"Now, Lizzy, you know we were going to drive out early. I have the perfect solution, though..."

Elizabeth Halloran had not held out against Brandon's wiles for months without having a well-developed stubborn streak of her own. "We will pick her up, Brandon." She patted Penny's hand. "It won't be a bit of trouble, dear. What time can you get off?"

Oddly disappointed, Penny said, "I suppose I could arrange to leave by four."

"Wonderful! That will be just fine, won't it, Brandon?"

Her grandfather looked as if he wanted to protest, but he finally heaved a sigh of resignation. "If it's what you want."

Elizabeth Halloran beamed at him as if he'd bestowed a special gift of diamonds on her. "Thank you, dear."

He shook his head. "Don't know how you do it, woman. I'll swear my mind's made up about something and next thing you know I'm agreeing to do the exact opposite. I thought marriage was supposed to be a compromise."

"It is," her grandmother said sweetly, linking her arm through his. "And you do it very well."

Chapter Six

The message at the top of the stack on Sam's desk was succinct. *A weekend at the Cape. Be there by seven on Friday. Dana.*

Without glancing at his calendar or giving it a second thought, he automatically reached for the phone and called his sister at work. While he waited for her secretary to pick up, he continued shuffling through the rest of the messages. It took a dozen or more rings, but Dana finally answered herself, sounding breathless and distracted.

Sam didn't even waste time on hello or asking why she was picking up her own phone. He just announced, "You know I can't get away from here on the weekend."

"Hello to you, too," she retorted. "Not good enough. That's what you've said every other time I asked."

"Because it's been true every other time you asked. Gang warfare doesn't take the weekend off. In fact, that's when things tend to really get out of hand. Something bad's coming down. I can feel it. We're barely into summer and the kids are already getting restless."

The comment was greeted with silence. Sam knew instinctively what she was thinking. She was worried and fighting to keep from letting it show.

"And you have to be in the middle of it?" she asked finally, wearily.

"I have to do what I can to keep these kids from killing each other," he countered patiently.

It was a familiar argument and they both had their parts down pat. By now they were pretty much going through the motions. He wondered why she'd even bothered with the invitation. It must have been a slow day at Halloran Industries.

"Not this time," Dana said.

Something in her voice alerted Sam that his big sister meant business. No matter how she worried about him, she rarely took a stand when it came to interfering with his job. When she did, she pulled out all the stops. He braced himself for whatever heavy artillery she planned to fire.

"Your niece, your *goddaughter,* is celebrating her tenth birthday at her grandparents' house and she wants you at the party. You *will* be at her party."

Her tone left no room for argument. The shot she'd fired was a good one, all right. Guilt sliced through him. "Hell, Dana, you know I would be if—"

"Oh, no," she said, cutting him off. "No ifs. You missed last year and the year before that and the year before that. You always have a good reason. She'll be old enough to go to college before you run out of excuses. This time I'm not taking no for an answer. You'll break her heart."

Sam envisioned Beth's huge blue eyes filled with tears of disappointment and something flipped over inside him.

"Doesn't she know she shouldn't count on me?" he muttered under his breath. He'd spent his whole life trying to make sure nobody counted on him. But even though he'd tried hard to steel himself against attachments of any sort, he had a soft spot in his heart for his sister's first child, his goddaughter with the golden hair, angelic smile and mischievous twinkle in her eyes.

With something akin to a fierce ache in his chest, he recalled the chaotic day Beth had been born as if it were yesterday. Dana's untimely labor pains had arrived only moments after she and Jason and Kevin and Lacey had renewed their wedding vows. Granddad Brandon had married his long-cherished love, Elizabeth Forsythe Newton, in the same ceremony. When Dana had announced that the baby didn't intend to wait for the cutting of the cake, the whole family had trouped to the hospital for the joyous event.

Sam recalled vividly the outpouring of love in his sister's hospital room after the birth. He'd never experienced anything like it before or since. Nor had he ever felt more alone. With the birth of that baby, his sister had solidified her place in that huge, loving family. But no matter how he'd been welcomed into the fold, they hadn't been *his* family. They never would be. Not really.

His family consisted of a father who'd cut them loose, never to be seen again, and a mother who'd never recovered from his departure, dying a short time later. Sam knew a lot about abandonment and very little about commitment. Even his devoted sister had moved on to a new life, a life she deserved.

"Sis, don't let her rely on me," he said. "I'm a lousy bet when it comes to stuff like this."

"Too late. She does count on you and that's that," Dana retorted. "She's a smart kid who adores her uncle. She thinks you're handsome and brave and just this once you will not let her down."

Sam knew when he was beaten. The drive would be a killer, but maybe he could get to Cape Cod long enough for the birthday party at least. "What time's the party?"

"Be out at Lacey and Kevin's by seven on Friday."

There was something a little vague about the reply that worried him. "Is that when the party's planned?" he asked suspiciously.

"Just show up and don't plan on leaving until Sunday night."

"Dana! Didn't you hear a word I said?"

"Every one of them. This time, though, you're going to pay more attention to your family than you do to those hellions on the streets," she declared, an unexpected trace of anger in her voice.

Before he could protest the unfairness of that, she hung up on him. As usual, she had gotten the last word. It was probably just as well. Anything he might have said would have been a lie.

Dana was right. He didn't pay nearly enough attention to either his sister or her children. After all she'd done for him, he figured one weekend out of his life wasn't such a big price to pay. But Cape Cod? For an entire weekend? He'd be bored by bedtime on Friday and there would still be two endless days stretching out ahead of him.

He wondered if Dana steamrolled over Jason the same way she'd just hoodwinked him. Of course, judging from the adoration on her husband's face, Dana merely had to whisper her slightest desire and Jason would travel the globe if necessary trying to fulfill it. They had a good marriage, a rock-solid marriage.

Sam wondered what the odds were of that happening for a kid whose father had vanished and whose mother had died of a broken heart. A hundred to one? More like a million to one. Dana was the one in a million who'd lucked out. He'd always figured that lightning couldn't possibly strike twice. He'd go through life solo before he'd risk a lousy marriage. Everyone knew cops were bad bets. Lousy schedules, low pay, constant fear. And occasionally they wound up dead. All of it guaranteed misery for the women who loved them. He wouldn't do to some women what his father had done to his mother. He wouldn't leave her to struggle through an uncertain future alone, maybe even to raise his kids alone.

Getting time off had been amazingly easy. Apparently Sam wasn't nearly as indispensable as he liked to think he was. In fact, his boss had said something to the effect that it was about time he'd decided to take a break, that tired cops made mistakes.

So there was to be no salvation from that direction, he thought ruefully. He had his three days off.

That Friday by the time he arrived on Cape Cod, he was already dreading the endless hours with nothing to do. Endless hours closed up in a house with three little munchkins, albeit adorable ones. He shuddered at the thought of it. He figured he'd last through lunch on Saturday before he lost it and tore back to the city, disappointing Beth and infuriating Dana.

When he pulled into the driveway of the cozy beachfront cottage where Kevin and Lacey Halloran lived year-round now, he drew in a deep breath and willed himself to get into the spirit of the occasion.

Before he could solidify his resolve, the front door flew open and Beth raced out. Obviously she considered herself to be hostess to any arrival. The expression of delight that spread across her face when she saw him more than made up for his reluctance to come. All at once he felt as if some great weight had been lifted from his shoulders, even though there was something a little scary about being loved so unconditionally.

"Uncle Sam, you're here! You're really here. Mom said you were coming, but I was so afraid something would happen."

Chubby arms circled his waist. He glanced over her blond head and met Dana's eyes. She grinned unrepentantly, her I-told-you-so look.

He picked the ten-year-old up, groaned dramatically and set her down again. "It's true," he complained. "You are definitely grown up. What happened to the little kid I could toss in the air without breaking my back?"

"You saw me at Easter, Uncle Sam. It's only June. I haven't grown that much since then," Beth protested.

"Must be the light, then. You look like a young lady."

She giggled and clutched his hand. "Did you bring a present?" She glanced at her mother and hurriedly amended the question. "You didn't have to."

"Oh, in that case, maybe I'll take it back."

Worried blue eyes met his. "No, please. What is it?"

He grinned at her. "It wouldn't be a surprise if I told you, would it?"

"I guess not. Wait till you see who's here. Even Great-Grandpa flew in. He said it was a very special occasion and he had to be here," she said, obviously brimming over with self-importance.

Sam's gaze shot to Dana. "Brandon's here?"

She nodded. "And Elizabeth."

He couldn't quite identify the feeling that stole over him. "I suppose that means Penny will be here, too?" he asked, hoping he sounded more nonchalant than he felt.

Dana chuckled. "Did you imagine we could leave out any member of the family within a hundred-mile radius?"

"Does she know I'm coming?"

"I didn't discuss the guest list with her, if that's what you're asking."

Sam's stomach knotted. It was definitely going to be a long weekend, though he supposed it was far better that she was here rather than back in Boston where he'd be worrying about her running into Tank. Here he'd only have to worry about keeping his own hands off of her. It ought to be an interesting test of his willpower. He glanced at Dana and saw that she was regarding him with evident curiosity.

"Something up between you and Penny? I didn't realize you knew each other that well."

"Not as well as Granddad Brandon would like," he retorted, leaving his own misguided desires out of it. "It promises to be a very long weekend."

His sister's lips twitched. A twinkle sparked in her eyes. "You're kidding?"

"I wish I were."

"Amazing."

"What's so amazing about it? The man certainly did his share of meddling to assure you and Jason got together."

"No. I meant it's amazing that Penny's never said a word to me about it."

This time it was his turn to be startled. "You've seen her?"

"We've talked on the phone a couple of times. We've been trying to get together for lunch but our schedules haven't meshed yet."

"And my name hasn't come up?"

She grinned at him. "Disappointed, little brother?"

"No. I'm just surprised."

Her expression sobered. "I like her, you know. She's got a lot of spunk."

"Spunk? That's not the description I would use."

"Oh? What would you use?"

He thought about it for a minute, instantly envisioning that honey shade of her hair, the silkiness of her skin, the imagined warmth of her lips beneath his. He sure as hell wasn't about to mention any of that. Apparently his silence had gone on too long. Dana was watching him speculatively.

"I see," she said with obvious amusement. "She's left you dumbstruck."

"Oh, for heaven's sake, don't *you* start," he muttered. "Let's get inside. I want some birthday cake."

"Then you're in for a disappointment," she said, linking her arm through his. "The party's not till Sunday."

"You brat!" he accused, laughing as he tossed her over his shoulder and carried her into the house.

Just inside the door, he ran smack into Penny. She shook her head as she looked from him to Dana and back again. He got the feeling she was recalling the way he'd recently carted her around the same way.

"Must be some caveman thing," she commented dryly, but her eyes were sparkling with laughter.

She was wearing shorts that exposed surprisingly long, shapely legs and a halter top that would have been banned by the Boston city fathers if she'd worn it on the streets there. For an instant Sam forgot all about his wriggling sister, who was pummeling him and demanding to be let down. His breath lodged in his chest and left him disgustingly tongue-tied. This thunderbolt effect Penny Hayden had on him was bad, very bad, he told himself.

And it was only the beginning of three days of pure, sweet torment.

Penny had guessed that Sam would be on the Cape for the weekend. She'd told herself that his presence wouldn't make a bit of difference. She'd handle it like a mature adult, avoiding him when at all possible. He'd probably be delighted to help her out with that, glad to leave her to the other almost instinctive bodyguards in the Halloran clan. Their paths wouldn't even have to cross except at meals.

That plan did not take into account the possibility of rain. When the skies opened up about eight o'clock Friday night, it sent them all scrambling indoors with their plates of clams and coleslaw and their iced mugs of beer. The house was large enough to accommodate a lot of Hallorans, but it couldn't give the same illusion of privacy that Penny could achieve at an outdoor clambake. In fact, with all of them crowded around the dining-room table, it was downright cozy and intimate. Lacey had insisted on lighting the room with old-fashioned hurricane lanterns, which created an all-too-romantic ambience.

It didn't help that somehow Sam had allowed himself to be maneuvered into the chair next to hers. His leg, bare below a pair of faded cut-off jeans, brushed against hers...and didn't budge. The only way she could retreat would be to shove her grandfather aside or leave the table entirely. Either choice would be telling, an admission of something she wasn't prepared to acknowledge. And she knew her grandfather well enough to recognize that he would seize her actions as evidence to make his case for throwing her and Sam together nonstop until something happened between them.

Determined to give the impression that she wasn't the least bit fazed by the man next to her, Penny stayed where she was and tried to concentrate on her meal. She dutifully forked a clam into her mouth, then another. As a distraction, it failed miserably. She might as well have been eating sawdust.

At the same time, she could have described precisely the scent of Sam's soap—sandalwood, the texture of his skin—faintly rough but intriguingly warm, and the number of golden hairs scattered enticingly across the back of his hand—a dozen. Maybe more, she admitted. She'd started envisioning his hand on her flesh and lost count. Heat radiated through her in outrageously wicked waves. Embarrassment quickly followed.

"Excuse me," she mumbled. She shoved her chair away from the table and made a run for it.

She heard conversation grind to a halt, then a muttered comment, and the slow rise of voices again. No doubt they were speculating like mad about her abrupt departure. By then, though, she was outside, oblivious to what they might be saying, oblivious even to the chill of the rain that immediately drenched her. Given her overheated state of mind, she was surprised steam wasn't rising from her skin.

"You okay?"

Sam's smoky voice curled around her. She shivered—from the cold or from his sudden nearness, she couldn't say for sure. She chided herself for failing to hear him coming, for not having guessed that he would follow, whether of his own volition or as an emissary of her grandfather's.

"Penny?"

"I'm fine. I just needed some air."

"I suppose you've noticed that the rain is coming down in buckets."

"It feels good," she countered, unable to stop the shudder that swept through her. She wrapped her arms around her middle with the vague hope that he wouldn't notice how cold she was.

"Of course it feels wonderful," he said dryly. "There's nothing like an evening shower to invigorate a person. Of course, the temperature's probably dropped to fifty. Some people might consider that a warning."

"Oh?" she said, glancing his way. He was studiously avoiding her gaze, staring instead toward the pounding surf just beyond them. His shirt was soaked and plastered to his skin in a way that detailed every muscular inch of his chest. He didn't act as if he'd noticed.

"Pneumonia weather," he explained.

"I'm made of sturdy stuff. I'll be fine. You go on in if you're cold," she said, knowing it was wishful thinking on her part that he would leave. She had a hunch that Sam Roberts always finished what he started. Lord knows, he was stubborn as a mule.

"I'm not cold," he said. "But I am wondering what would send a perfectly rational person out into a night like this."

"I told you I needed some air."

"And the sky is green."

She lost the slim hold she'd had on her self-control and whirled on him. "Oh, don't be so damned smug."

"Smug?" he repeated. "What's that supposed to mean?"

Once she'd started hurling accusations, Penny couldn't seem to stop. "You know perfectly well that putting you and me into the same room is like leaving paint and turpentine in a garage, then casually tossing in a match. We've agreed that neither one of us wants to be involved in the resulting conflagration. You don't like me. You never have, which makes this chemistry or whatever it is all the more ridiculous."

Something in his eyes suddenly turned dark and dangerous. "Who said I didn't like you?" he asked softly.

Fortunately, thanks to the rain, he would probably never see the telltale tears tracking down her cheeks. "Some things you don't have to admit," she retorted. Years of silly heartbreak were in her voice. "Some things are just painfully obvious."

"Is that so?"

He reached toward her then and brushed a damp strand of hair from her face. Penny swayed into the touch. His fingers lingered on her cheek, his caress a warm and gentle counterpoint to the pounding rain. Penny actually felt her heart come to a complete standstill, then start again with the impossible force of thunder in her chest.

"What are you doing?" she asked, her voice shaky.

"I wish to hell I knew," he muttered as he slowly lowered his head until their breath mingled in the chilly night air.

"Sam?" Penny murmured wonderingly. This wasn't what she'd anticipated at all. Or was it? Maybe it had always been inevitable. At any rate, she felt as if she might faint dead away before he closed that infinitesimal distance between them.

"Hmm?"

"If you back out now, I will never forgive you."

"Sweetheart, I couldn't back out now if the entire family threatened to hang me at dawn."

Despite herself, despite the deliciously sweet tension of the moment, Penny chuckled at the image.

"Somehow I don't think that will be a problem," she murmured dryly just as Sam's mouth slanted softly over hers.

Chapter Seven

At first touch Penny's lips felt like ice under Sam's. His goal became to warm them, to learn the shape and texture of her mouth and imprint it indelibly in his brain so that he could recall it on cold, lonely nights. Soft as velvet, moist from the rain and tentative as a virgin's, her lips trembled beneath his.

Then she gave herself up to the intoxicating power of the kiss and he was lost. Sam knew all about technique and foreplay, but there was something sweetly innocent in the way Penny sighed and melted into his embrace. At the first tentative foray of her tongue, his heart slammed against his chest. He showed her how to deepen the kiss and like an apt and willing pupil, she studiously followed his lead with explosive results.

Sam wondered if she had any idea at all of the effect she was having on him. She gave a soft little whimper of pleasure when he tried to shift positions, molding herself to him in a way that guaranteed she wouldn't mistake exactly how hard he was. If she was shocked, though, it didn't show. She remained totally, enthusiastically committed to the kiss that was slowly driving him wild.

She tasted of butter and wine. Her warmed, soft-as-silk flesh gave off the old-fashioned sweet scent of primroses. He found it all breathtaking and faintly alarming.

Why the hell hadn't he guessed it would still be like this after all this time? Or maybe that was the point. He had guessed, and he'd done his damnedest to avoid having it come to this. He hadn't wanted to start something that would only come to a very bad end. That unwillingness to play with fire had probably been the one and only noble act of his entire life.

Sam never should have allowed his resolve to waver. But when she had gazed up at him with those tear-filled blue eyes and declared that she knew he didn't like her, her hurt had wrenched his heart. He'd reacted instinctively, wanting to comfort, wanting to prove her wrong, *needing* her in a way that scared the living daylights out of him and ought to flat-out terrify her. She didn't act terrified, though. She acted like a woman just discovering her sensuality and reveling in it.

He told himself that one kiss meant nothing. It would reassure her. It would satisfy this vague longing he always felt around her. It would put an end to the wondering. And then they could both go on about their business.

Yeah, right! That was like saying a tornado blew through town, destroying everything in its wake, but life went on as usual. Ho-hum.

Nothing—*nothing* would be the same after this, Sam thought wearily as he forced himself to pull away. Facing life alone would be harder than ever now that he knew exactly how much he was giving up.

Penny's eyes were fixed on him, her expression slightly dazed. He knew how she felt. He was feeling a little shaky himself. No, he corrected, a lot shaky. The wondering had been child's play compared to the unforgettable and wildly sensual reality.

"So much for that theory," he said, trying to inject a cavalier note into his voice.

"Which theory is that?" she murmured.

She was still regarding him in a way that made him feel like a movie star, a Super Bowl champion and an Olympic gold medalist all rolled into one. He lost his train of thought. "What?"

"You said something about a theory."

He suddenly decided it was best not to remind her of exactly what had sparked that kiss. He'd meant to prove only that he didn't dislike her. Instead he had a feeling he'd proven something a lot more dangerous and it would be better for both of them if she didn't guess what it was. Penny was the kind of woman who'd take that vulnerability and cling to it, turning it into an admission of love, into the forerunner of a commitment he was incapable of making.

He shrugged. "Never mind. We're both soaked. I think we'd better get back inside. Besides, I'm sure everyone is wondering what happened to us."

A smile tugged at her exceptionally kissable lips. "Do you really think they'll miss us? This is the most self-contained group of people I've ever known. I know I'm related to them, but sometimes I feel like such an outsider."

Sam regarded her with a vague sense of astonishment. "You do?"

"Of course, I do. It's not like I grew up with them, except for Grandmother. The rest of them were sprung on me when Brandon tracked down Grandmother and then everyone found out that my mother was really his daughter, the product of their incredible love affair before he went off to war. I was a teenager and I guess I found it all pretty exciting and romantic in a lot of ways, but it's definitely required some adjustment on all our parts."

"It happened a long time ago," Sam reminded her.

"Still, I remember that it took months for my mom and my Aunt Kate to overcome the realization that they were only half sisters. It must have been terrible for Kevin, too. Sometimes even now I see the way he looks at me and I just know he must still be struggling to accept the fact that my mother is his half sister, that I'm his niece and he never even knew about us until I was half-grown."

Sam recognized that what she said was true. Of all of the Hallorans, Kevin had had the most difficulty accepting the discovery that his father had another child. It hadn't helped that Brandon had bulldozed over his feelings as if they didn't matter. Kevin had seethed with resentment for months, until Lacey had finally interceded and smoothed things over.

For Sam the drama had unfolded at a safe emotional distance. Now, though, he could see for himself how out-of-place Penny might feel. And he could certainly empathize with her yearning to fit in.

"Is that why you decided to come to Boston to get your graduate degree, so you could get to know this side of your family better?"

Penny hesitated in a way that he found faintly troubling. There was a vague hint of something that might have been guilt in her eyes before she looked away. He wondered what that was all about. Had she had some ulterior motive in coming East? He couldn't imagine it. She struck him as one of the most open and honest women he'd ever met, but then, how well did he really know her?

"Penny," he prodded, "did you come here to get to know the rest of your family?"

"That was one of the reasons," she said finally, still evading his eyes. "And, of course, there was the allure of an Ivy League school. It will open a lot of doors eventually."

Sam sensed that she was leaving something important out of the explanation, but whatever it was she obviously didn't intend to reveal it to him. He felt the tug of some unspoken mystery pulling at him, but dismissed it as a cop's instinctive reaction to unanswered questions, nothing more dire than that.

He held out his hand. "Come on, Ms. Hayden, let's go back and face the music."

She regarded him quizzically, but she trustingly tucked her hand in his. "Face the music?"

"Your grandmother's worried looks. My sister's speculative glances. Grandfather's smug satisfaction."

She grinned. "I see what you mean."

They had reached the back door by then. Oddly reluctant to end what had been begun on the beach, Sam said, "We could give them something to talk about."

An impish gleam lit her eyes. "I could go slamming into the house swearing that I will never speak to you again as long as I live."

"That's one possibility," Sam agreed. "It's not the one I had in mind."

Before she could say anything, he pulled her back into his arms, slanted his mouth across hers and spent the next sixty seconds indulging another one of those dangerous whims of his. They were both breathless and a little stunned when he finally broke it off.

"That ought to do it," he murmured.

Penny nodded sagely. "It sure should. Now grandfather won't let up until he has us married."

With a wink, she turned and walked into the house, leaving him to wonder if he'd recognized those very probable consequences when he'd hauled her into his arms.

"What the devil's the matter with you, boy?" Brandon asked Sam on Saturday afternoon. The sun was blazing and everyone was on the beach enjoying a picnic. Sam had remained on the back deck, alone with his beer and his muddled thoughts.

"You've been jumpy all day," Brandon observed. "Looks to me like you didn't sleep a wink all night, either. Something on your mind?"

Sam scowled at him. "What could be on my mind?" he inquired testily. He knew exactly where they were heading with this conversation. He'd been expecting it all morning long. The fact that it had taken Brandon until well past lunchtime to get him alone had left him feeling more jittery than a teenager facing an indignant father after a first date.

"Thought maybe you were thinking about Penny," Brandon said.

He affected a look of supreme innocence that made Sam want to grind his teeth. "Why would you think that?"

"You two seem to be getting . . . closer."

"So?"

"Don't make me spell it out for you, son."

Sam glared at him. "Now what is that supposed to mean?"

"If you hurt her, I'll never forgive you."

"Then why the hell did you insist on throwing us together in the first place?"

"Because it seemed to me you'd make a good match."

"But if we don't, it's going to be my fault?"

"Hell, son, if you can't see what's right in front of your eyes, then yes, it's your own damned fault," he snapped impatiently.

"Isn't there one other single person in the world whose life you can meddle in?"

Brandon didn't seem to be the least bit upset by the pointed question. "I suppose I could find somebody, but there's no one I care about more than the two of you."

"I'm all wrong for her," Sam retorted. "Why can't you see that?"

"If you're so wrong for her, then you had no business kissing her."

"And you had no business spying on us."

"Hell, boy, you were standing right at the back door in the pouring rain. Who could miss it? That's not the point, anyway."

"What *is* the point?"

"You've been selling yourself short. Always have. You've got a good head and, more important, a good heart. All you need is the right woman."

"And you think your granddaughter is that woman," he said, his voice flat.

Brandon grinned at him. "Doesn't matter a hill of beans what I think. My gut tells me you *know* she's the right woman. Don't wait too long to admit it to yourself and to her."

"How can you say that? She drives me crazy. I make her crazy."

Brandon chuckled. "I know. Ain't love grand?"

Sam was avoiding her. Penny had expected it, but that didn't stop it from hurting. Obviously he was regretting the kisses, regretting the fragile intimacy that had sprung up between them on the beach the night before.

Well, no matter what happened, she wasn't going to waste time on regrets. Those kisses had been the most magical, eye-popping, wicked events in her entire life and she intended to treasure them. She knew their importance, even if Sam refused to acknowledge it. Unlike that bittersweet kiss years ago, these had been filled with tenderness and real emotion.

"Don't let him get to you," Dana advised, joining her on the beach.

"Who?"

"My brother."

At that moment, Sam, Jason, Kevin and even Brandon had joined in a noisy game of inept volleyball with Dana's kids. Penny's gaze seemed to be riveted to Sam's sleekly muscled body as he held two-year-old Jason Junior in the air to smack a ball over the net. Penny sighed.

"You've got it bad, don't you?" Dana said.

"I hardly know him." The denial was perfunctory at best. She didn't honestly expect Dana to believe it. Judging from her grin, she didn't.

"Sometimes time has nothing to do with it."

"We've never gotten along."

"Nobody ever gets along with Sam, if he has his way. That's how he protects himself from getting hurt. Can I give you a word of advice?"

"Why not?"

"Don't pay any attention to what he says. Watch what he does. You know the kind of life we had before Jason came along. Everything was a struggle. We'd lost both my parents. All we had to depend on was each other. Then I went off and married Jason. As much as we try to make Sammy a part of our life, he's always felt like he lost me, too. So, he tries to stay away. He tries not to feel anything for any of us. He figures if he makes the wall high enough and thick enough, he'll never be hurt or abandoned again."

Dana's words made perfect sense, but they left Penny feeling more unsure of herself than ever. She regarded Sam's sister wistfully. "You know what's on the other side of that wall, because you've had a lifetime to understand him. He lets you see what's going on inside him, because he trusts you. How do I get beyond it?"

"Time. Patience. Love. You have to love him enough to look beyond the wall."

Easier said than done, Penny thought as Dana went off to join in the volleyball game. Anyway, who had said anything about love? Besides the incurably romantic Didi, of course.

Penny was willing to admit she was attracted to Sam, sufficiently attracted to him that she'd been inevitably drawn back to Boston to do her graduate work after years of refusing invitations to visit. That was what she had been longing to tell him the night before, but she had known that he wasn't ready for that much honesty. She'd stayed away as long as she could and when her silly, childish fantasies about him hadn't died, she had come back to discover why.

Maybe it had been her stubborn pride at stake, too. Sam was the first important person in her entire life who hadn't immediately and without reservation liked her. She'd had doting parents, supportive sisters, a generous aunt, an adoring grandmother and then an even more adoring grandfather. Her teachers thought she was brilliant. She'd grown up surrounded by friends.

And then, along had come Sam Roberts, the first boy she'd seriously fallen for, and he'd rejected her as little more than a pesky nuisance to be tolerated out of some sense of duty. It had shaken her self-esteem more than she would have ever thought possible. Maybe if it had come at any other time in her life, it wouldn't have mattered so much. But she had been sixteen, discovering what love was all about for the very first time. And Sam was someone her grandfather admired and respected. It made his opinion of her count for even more.

Other young men had followed that first disastrous encounter with Sam. She had been very popular her senior year in high school and all through college. No Friday or Saturday night passed without a date. But few dates were repeated and no one had made her feel the same way Sam had—good or bad.

She'd never been naive enough to believe she would go through life beloved by every single person on earth, but she hadn't had a lot of practice with rejection. Something in Sam's attitude had made her want desperately to prove that whatever assumptions he had made about her were wrong. She refused to accept the possibility that it was just a case of oil and water not mixing. Plus not one single kiss in her entire dating experience had wiped out the yearning she felt for the one kiss that had never happened.

And now that it had happened? She was going to figure out some way to fight Sam's stubbornness, some way to make sure that last night's kisses weren't the only ones they ever shared. If Grandfather and everyone else wanted to throw them together, including the troublesome Tank Landry, so much the better. She no longer intended to put up any kind of fuss whatsoever. She'd take all the help she could get.

Maybe what she felt for Sam wasn't love. But whatever it was was more intriguing than anything she had ever felt before and she didn't intend to give it up without a fight.

Unwilling to join in the volleyball game and still trying to sort out her thoughts, Penny stood and started down the beach. Maybe a long walk would clear her head. It was a spectacular day, a stunning contrast to the previous night's deluge. The sky had been washed clean by the rain, the deep blue of the Atlantic was topped by perfect whitecaps, and the crisp breeze was counterpointed by the sun's warmth.

Penny walked for an hour or more, lost in thought, feeling oddly contented, as if a major decision in her life had finally been made. She was heading back when she saw Sam jogging along the beach, kicking up water behind him, his body hard from regular workouts at the gym. She envied him his easy gait and even more, his ease with his own body. She'd always felt slightly awkward and definitely not the least bit athletic.

He slowed when he saw her. "You've been gone awhile."

Inordinately pleased that he'd noticed, she responded with a careless shrug. "I felt like a long walk."

"You should have joined us at volleyball. We could have used the help."

"I'm too short. I can't get the ball over the net to save my soul. Every year in high school physical education there was a unit on volleyball and every year I was totally humiliated."

"We're not talking world peace here. It's supposed to be fun."

"It's not fun if everyone laughs at you."

"Tomorrow, after everyone rests up, we'll show you our version of the game. If the two-year-old can participate, you can play. He's much shorter than you are."

"He had an advantage. He was sitting on your shoulders."

"Tomorrow it's your turn."

"My turn to do what?"

"You'll sit on my shoulders."

Apparently oblivious to the effect that suggestion had on her, he turned and fell into step beside her. She tamed her pulse and tried to keep any hint of breathlessness out of her voice. "I thought you were going for a run."

"Just stretching my legs." He looked down at her. "Your nose is sunburned. Didn't you put any lotion on it?"

Penny winced. "I forgot. It's in my pocket." She pulled out the tube.

"It doesn't do you any good in there." He held out his hand. When he had the tube, he squeezed out a dab on his finger, then slowly rubbed it on her nose.

Whether it was caused by the chill of the lotion or Sam's gentle touch, Penny shivered. She lifted her gaze to meet his. He was intent on what he was doing, his brow furrowed in concentration. With the pad of his thumb, he smoothed the lotion across her cheeks, then trailed his fingers along her jaw.

At some point, and Penny wasn't entirely certain when, the caress changed. It no longer had anything to do with the application of suntan lotion and everything to do with the simple touch of his fingers against her skin.

His gaze finally met hers. He looked so confused, so utterly uncertain, that Penny wanted to promise him that everything was going to be all right. Unfortunately, with her breath lodged in her throat and her pulse hammering, she wasn't so sure it was true. She

had the distinct feeling that she and Sam Roberts were
headed for trouble.

Unlike Sam, though, she could hardly wait to get
there.

Chapter Eight

Randy was pacing up and down the street outside the gym when Sam arrived for his Monday workout. He'd been looking forward to it all day, counting on it to relieve the frustration that had built up in him throughout the weekend on Cape Cod. He hadn't held out a lot of hope it would work, but it was the only thing he could think of to try that wouldn't just complicate an already complex situation.

"Where have you been, man?" Randy demanded. "I've been looking all over. I even went to the police station."

The near panic in the boy's voice didn't worry Sam nearly as much as his visit to the police station. Randy wouldn't have gone there except in a dire emergency.

"I was away for the weekend. What's up?" he asked, trying to keep his voice even so that his own alarm wouldn't show. Randy already appeared to be on the edge.

"Tank and the guys, they've been talking a lot about your girl."

It was the last thing Sam needed to hear. He'd wanted desperately to push Penny out of his mind tonight.

"She is not *my girl*," he snapped. He attributed his sour mood to a handful of kisses that might have gotten out of hand if he hadn't kept a tight rein on his libido. Unfortunately he was now paying the price for being so blasted honorable. Randy's reminder that Penny could have been his girl in the most basic way possible was untimely at best.

Randy regarded him with astonishment. "She's not?"

"No, she is not," he said firmly, trying not to think of the way she had melted in his arms, of the way her body had fit his as if they'd been made for each other.

"Well, whatever. The point is that Tank thinks she is. I think he's planning to put some moves on her." He regarded Sam worriedly. "You know what I'm saying?"

Sam's blood came to a slow boil. He'd been expecting something like this, but the reality of it filled him with outrage.

"I understand," he said slowly, determined not to let his temper get the best of him. He had to think rationally, go strictly by the book. "When?"

"I don't know. Soon, I guess. He doesn't say much around me, you know, because he knows you and me are pals. But the other guys, they let it slip."

Sam realized what it must have taken for Randy to risk telling him. He wondered if the boy understood the significance of the choice he'd made. "Why are you warning me?"

"Because you've tried to be my friend. I figure I owe you. And I don't like the things they were talking about. Ms. Hayden looks like a nice lady. I wouldn't want to see her hurt that way. It's wrong. It's not like taking some jewelry or a TV or something. I'd keep an eye on her, if I were you. I mean, if you care."

Sam cared. Despite his protests, that much was undeniable. He cared more than he should, more than he wanted to. He thought of the undercover surveillance he was scheduled to be on all night. Then he thought of Penny's habit of walking everywhere she went. Damn! Maybe he could send Jason to pick her up after work, but how the devil would he explain that to either of them? And switching duty with one of the other cops would raise just as many questions. It looked as if he was going to have to trust Randy, at least for the next few hours until he could get off duty.

"You busy tonight?" he asked.

The teenager shrugged. "Nothing I can't get out of."

"I want you to get over to the lab where Penny works. You know where that is?"

Randy nodded. "I've followed her there with Tank and the guys a couple of times."

Sam decided not to comment on that. For the moment, he was glad Randy had been around Tank to hear what the punk had in mind.

He put his hand on Randy's shoulder. "Okay, here's what I need you to do. Wait around until she leaves, then stick close to her until she gets home. If one of your pals comes within eyesight, I want you to beep me. Don't take any chances. Beep me the minute Tank shows up."

"Should I let her know what I'm doing?"

Sam thought of Penny's insistence that she could take care of herself without any interference from him. "The lady likes to think she can take on the world. Let's let her go on thinking that. Just don't let her out of your sight."

Randy straightened his shoulders. "You can trust me, Sam. I'll make sure she's safe."

Sam nodded. "I appreciate it. I'll be by as soon as I can shake loose from my assignment. If you need me sooner, though, beep me."

"I promise."

Sam shook his hand. "Thanks for warning me about this. I owe you one."

Randy grinned shyly. "Nah, man. I owe you. It means a lot knowing you'd trust me."

He turned and trotted off in the direction of the bus stop. As he watched him go, Sam prayed that his trust in the boy wasn't misplaced. *Come on, Roberts,* he told himself sternly. *The kid came to warn you, didn't he?*

But when push came to shove, would Randy's allegiance go to the cop who'd befriended him or to the gang members he'd known his whole life? Sam debated calling off the surveillance and going to keep an eye on Penny himself. Surely, though, for this one night at least, she would be safe enough in Randy's hands. He could be there himself in a few hours. In the meantime, he would be only minutes away if anything came down and Randy alerted him. He had to believe that would give him enough time.

In the end, though, it was the longest five hours of his life. By the time midnight finally rolled around, he couldn't wait to cross town and relieve Randy from his watch over Penny's building.

Unfortunately, when he pulled up outside, he saw no sign of the teenager. Nor was there a single light burning in Penny's apartment. It was possible she had gone to bed, but if so, where the hell was Randy? He should have been on the street somewhere keeping an eye on things.

Sam parked down the block, then crossed over to the entrance to her building. He checked the tiny lobby, then went back outside and slowly walked around the entire building, cursing the fact that Penny didn't have a car he could look for to determine if she was even home.

He was just heading back for his own car when his beeper went off.

"Damn! I knew it. I just knew it," he muttered as he took off running. He was already starting the engine as he used his cellular phone to dial the number that showed on his beeper.

Randy picked up on the first ring. "Sam, is that you? Man, you gotta get here. First, she went to the library. She was there for hours with this big pile of books. I think I must be allergic to dust or something. I was sneezing the whole time. Anyway, then she went for coffee with some woman. They've been yakking for the past hour or more. All of a sudden I see Tank and the guys coming down the block."

The words tumbled out so fast, it was all Sam could do to follow the gist. As soon as he heard Tank's name mentioned, he interrupted. "Where are you?"

Randy described an all-night diner a few miles away near the campus.

Sam slapped a flashing light on the roof of his car, hit the siren and squealed around the corner. "I'll be there in five minutes, tops."

"Should I go inside? Try to keep her there? She looks like she's getting ready to leave. She's getting money out of her purse to pay the check."

Sam considered the options. None of them were ideal. "Has Tank seen you?" he asked finally.

"No."

"But he has seen her?"

"Man, what do you think he's doing here?" Randy said impatiently. "This ain't his kinda place. All these intellectual dudes give him the creeps."

"Is he inside or outside?"

"They've been hanging around outside, but it looks like he's getting ready to go in."

"Is the place busy?"

"Not really. Just some lady waiting tables and some guy making burgers. Looks like three, maybe four people sitting at the counter. I can't see one end."

With any luck, that was enough witnesses to keep Tank from causing any real trouble inside the place. And hopefully Penny wouldn't budge once she'd seen Tank. She'd promised him that she wouldn't take foolish chances where the gang leader was concerned. And if the woman with her was Didi, she'd probably pressure her to keep her word.

"Stay where you are," Sam told him. "I need you where you can keep telling me what's happening without being seen. I'm maybe a mile away now. You should be hearing the siren."

"I think I hear it already," Randy said. "Maybe you should cut it, though. Tank gets real spooked when he hears one. He's liable to do something crazy."

"Crazy like what? Is he carrying?" he asked, already heeding Randy's advice and cutting the siren. He killed the light while he was at it. No point in alarming Tank.

"Not a gun," Randy said. "But he always has this knife. He's good with it, too."

Envisioning that knife held at Penny's throat made him sick to his stomach. Sam gripped the steering wheel until his knuckles turned white. He had to stay cool. He needed to stroll casually into the place and prevent anything from happening, rather than causing it. With that in mind, he managed to take the last corner on all four wheels. He slanted the car into the only available space on the block, ignoring the fire hydrant. There'd be hell to pay for that if a by-the-book beat cop came along.

He made himself sit in the car long enough to give Randy a final set of instructions. "Randy, I can see where you are. I want you to stay right by that phone. If things get out of hand inside, you call 9-1-1 for backup immediately. Just tell them an officer needs assistance. You understand?"

"Yeah. Are you sure you don't want me to come in with you, though?" he asked, obviously disappointed not to be included in whatever action was about to go down.

"No. You've handled this just fine. Now leave the rest to me, okay?"

"Sure, if you say so."

Sam observed Tank through the diner's window. He and his pals were seated one booth away from Penny and Didi Rogers. So far they were behaving like a regular group of guys stopping for a late-night soda. Even so, Sam felt a cold fury every time he thought about what they probably had on their minds.

He crossed the street slowly, careful not to look in Randy's direction. As he reached for the door, he drew in a last breath and prayed that he could pull this off without any bloodshed.

With his gaze fixed on Penny and her friend and a smile plastered on his face, he sauntered down the aisle. Penny glanced up and regarded him with a shocked expression.

"Hey, sweetheart," he said, leaning down to kiss her on the cheek as if meeting her here were a nightly occurrence. He nodded at Didi, who was grinning expectantly. Judging from the twinkle in her eyes, his name had come up in their conversation.

"What...?" Penny began.

Before she could complete the question, he covered her mouth with his own, lingering just a tad longer than was actually necessary for the effect he was trying to create. Nudging her over, he slid into the booth beside her. He squeezed her hand, hoping she'd respond to the warning.

She stayed quiet, but her whole body was tense with indignation. Knowing her, at any second all that irritation was going to spill out in the form of a very vocal explosion. To buy time, he gestured to the waitress for a cup of coffee, then waited until she'd brought it. Keeping his voice even, he told the two women, "We have company in the next booth."

"You mean Tank," Penny said without the least hint of concern in her voice.

"You saw him, then?"

"I'm not blind, for heaven's sake."

"Word on the street is that tonight's the night he plans to make good on his threat."

Her eyes widened at that. "Against me?"

"You've got it, sweetheart."

"Maybe if you'd stop calling me that, I wouldn't be in this fix."

"Too late now," he retorted, figuring it had been too late from the moment they'd met a long time ago. Penny was destined to be trouble for him, in one way or another.

Didi Rogers was regarding them curiously. "Anyone care to tell me what's going on?"

Before either of them could answer, Tank stood and made his way to their booth. He surveyed Didi appreciatively, cast a dismissive look at Sam, then turned his gaze on Penny. The kid's testosterone was clearly in overdrive.

"How come you want to hang around with a loser like him?" he asked, attempting to affect a mature derisiveness. Given his careless hairstyle, the zits on his face and his deliberately torn jeans, it was a futile effort.

Sam held his breath, praying Penny would keep her usual sass out of her response.

"He's dull," she admitted, looking Sam up and down. "But I do think he's cute."

Next to her, Sam seethed. Dull? *Dull?* He'd show her dull.

"I could show you a better time," Tank offered, then proceeded to enumerate an X-rated list of his major attributes.

Sam was on his feet in a heartbeat. He moved so quickly that Tank didn't have time to react. Before the fourth filthy word crossed his lips, Sam had him slammed against the wall with his arm twisted behind his back. It effectively cut off the flow of words.

"Apologize to the lady," he ordered.

"What for, man? The truth's the truth." His voice rose when Sam wrenched his arm higher. "Watch it, pal. You're making a case for police brutality. I got me a whole roomful of witnesses."

"I'm off duty," Sam advised him. "This is between you and me, man-to-man. Now I want you to apologize to the lady and then I want you and your friends to take off. It's way past your bedtime. If I see you anywhere near Ms. Hayden again, you'll regret the day you were born. Are we clear on that?"

"Clear as crystal," Tank replied in the high, squeaky voice that was all he could apparently manage while in extreme pain.

Suddenly Sam felt a gentle touch on his forearm and caught the scent of Penny's perfume. Primroses. How could anything so sweetly innocent be so damned arousing? This was no time for his body to be responding like some horny teenager's.

"I'm sure there won't be any more trouble," she said softly. She fastened her big blue eyes on Tank. "Will there, Tank?"

"No, ma'am," he said grudgingly.

A little of the fight seemed to drain out of him. Maybe she'd cast a spell on the kid, just as she had on him, Sam thought with a weary sense of resignation.

"Let him go," she said.

Even though Tank appeared to have lost interest in his previous plans for the night, Sam wanted him to know that one misstep was going to bring a whole lot of trouble down around him. "Penny, stay out of this, okay? Let me handle it," he said.

"And break that poor boy's arm? I don't think so."

Her gaze clashed with his. Her chin rose stubbornly. Sam wasn't sure whether to laugh or cry. Disgusted, he released Tank with a final shove toward the door.

Tank managed a smirk as he rubbed his arm. "It ain't over till it's over," he said smugly. He gestured toward his pals, who silently slid from the booth where they'd been watching the scene with a combination of fascination and worry. Apparently they hadn't been anxious to tangle with a cop, especially one as motivated as Sam appeared to be.

"You'd better hope it's over," Sam warned one last time. "Pretty boys like you don't fare so well in prison."

The words hung in the air as Tank took off, followed by his friends. For several minutes after they'd gone, there was dead silence in the diner, then everyone began talking at once. Sam sat back down, picked up his cup of now cold coffee and took a healthy swallow. He didn't want the coffee, but he wanted desperately to buy some time before he said one single word to the irritating, annoying, impossible woman sitting next to him.

"Did you really have to be so rough on him?" she said before he could rein in his temper. "And what was all that garbage about what would happen to him in prison? Were you trying to scare him to death?''

"Rough on him?" he repeated incredulously. "You do realize what he had in mind, don't you? And yes, I was trying to scare him to death."

Her eyes flared just a bit, but she waved off the implication. "He wouldn't have gone through with it. You said yourself that these boys just need someone to pay attention to them, give them a little self-esteem. Like your friend, Randy."

As if on cue, Randy wandered inside, his expression worried. "Everything okay?"

"Depends who you ask," Sam said sourly.

Didi regarded Penny with concern. "You might be acting just a little too nonchalant about this," she suggested. "That punk has the meanest eyes I've ever seen. He also has something to prove. That's a dangerous combination."

"Oh, come on. They're just boys," Penny said bravely, but the first tiny hint of doubt had made its way into her voice.

Sam gritted his teeth. When he could keep from shouting, he said, "Randy, Ms. Hayden believes that Tank and his buddies mean her no serious harm. Is that your reading of the situation?"

He shook his head. "No, ma'am. That's what I told Sam. I think they meant to hurt you real bad. I heard 'em talking myself."

Sam regarded her triumphantly. "See what I mean?"

She swallowed hard and this time there was no mistaking the uncertainty in her voice. "Tonight? You actually knew they meant to get me tonight? That's why you showed up? It wasn't just coincidence?"

"It was no coincidence. Randy kept an eye on you until I got off. He beeped me about thirty minutes ago and warned me it looked as if Tank meant to stir up some trouble in here."

"Then you arrived in the nick of time," Didi said, an approving gleam in her eyes. "I always did like heroes with a sense of timing."

Penny finally looked so thoroughly shaken that Sam relented and reached for her hand. It was ice cold. He rubbed it to warm the skin. "You okay?"

"Just peachy," she said with forced cheer.

"How about Randy and I escort the two of you home?"

"I think that would be a very good idea," Didi said, apparently not willing to leave it to Penny to make a wise decision on the subject.

Sam paid the check, then led the way to his car. When Penny climbed into the back beside Didi, he kept his mouth firmly shut. Randy got into the front passenger seat.

"Thanks for what you did tonight," he told the boy. "It's because of you that things never got out of hand."

"Anytime." He glanced shyly over the back seat toward Penny. "I've got some time on my hands, if you'd like me to hang out nearby for a while."

"I'd feel better if you would," Penny said to Sam's astonishment. Then he caught the look that passed between them and wondered who would really be watching out for whom. He had a hunch Penny had just found herself a stray to nurture. And he knew for a fact that it would be good for Randy to develop a sense of responsibility for someone other than himself.

They dropped off Didi first, then Randy. He asked to be let out on a street corner.

"Here?" Penny asked, looking around with obvious dismay as she got out of the back seat to take his seat in front.

"I'll be fine, ma'am. What time would you like me to come by in the morning?"

"About seven, if that's not too early."

"I'll be there," he promised.

He was still standing on the corner when they pulled away.

Penny regarded Sam worriedly. "Are you sure we should leave him out here all alone at this hour? Shouldn't we have taken him all the way to his doorstep? What if Tank comes after him?"

"I doubt he has a doorstep," Sam said matter-of-factly. "He's split from every foster home he's been placed in for the last four years. I have a hunch Johnny's been letting him sleep at the gym, but obviously Randy doesn't want either of us to know that. As for Tank, hopefully he never guessed Randy had anything to do with my sudden arrival tonight."

"He'd make him pay for that, wouldn't he?"

"In spades," Sam agreed.

"Oh, that poor boy," Penny murmured.

"Don't feel too sorry for him. You have more important things to worry about."

"Like?"

"Like where I'm going to sleep tonight."

Her gaze shot to his. "In your own bed, I assume."

"No way, sweetheart. The choices are the sofa in your living room or your bed."

"Oh, no. Forget it."

"Take your pick. I'm too tired to argue." He figured giving her a choice in the matter was yet another example of the sort of nobility she aroused in him. He figured he could have talked his way into her bed in five minutes flat, if he'd put his mind to it. Two minutes, if he'd kissed her again the way he had when they'd been standing on the beach in the pouring rain on Friday night. He waited expectantly for her answer.

Unfortunately for his peace of mind, she kept her mouth clamped firmly shut until they were all the way inside the apartment. She tore up the stairs and into the place as if she were Paul Revere trying to get the message out about the arrival of the British. Sam took heart from the fact that she was heading for her bedroom.

To his deep regret, she emerged just as quickly, her arms piled high with sheets and pillows. She dumped them unceremoniously on her sofa. Her sofa that was no more than five feet long. Her sofa that had the lumpiest cushions he'd ever set eyes on. He was cursing his fate and the general unpredictability of women when her bedroom door slammed with the force of a hurricane behind it.

He grinned, despite himself. "I guess next time, I'll have sense enough not to ask."

Chapter Nine

Penny couldn't get to sleep. Her blood raced as if she'd had ten cups of the strongest coffee available, rather than the one cup of decaf she'd nursed all evening. She told herself that any sensible woman would have been wide awake and tossing and turning after the close call she'd had tonight. Unfortunately, she knew that the episode with Tank had nothing to do with her insomnia. The potential of danger no doubt had been there, but in reality it had been a minor incident.

No, it was the presence of Sam Roberts in her living room that had her on edge. As infuriating as he could sometimes be, the man was more tempting than an entire pound of Belgian chocolates.

She told herself it wasn't as if this was the first time they'd slept under the same roof. They had just spent the entire weekend in the same house on Cape Cod. But there they had been surrounded by people, she reminded herself. Hell, who was she kidding? She hadn't slept a wink on the Cape, either, and for the very same reason. She wanted the man in her bed. Tonight he had offered to join her there. And she, for some reason she couldn't entirely fathom, had turned him down. Was she out of her mind or what?

Penny tried to sort out what had brought them to this point. The powerful, if somewhat innocent yearning she had felt at sixteen had turned into full-blown, weak-in-the-knees lust. After he'd kissed her the other night, it had only gotten worse. She had felt his desire and it had been just as overwhelming as her own. The fact that he seemed so damned determined not to admit that it meant anything only complicated matters. Obviously the challenge he'd uttered tonight—the sofa or her bed—had been a test. But for which one of them? she wondered.

Ten years ago, with the fragile ego of a sixteen-year-old just discovering her sexuality, she had taken his rejection personally. She'd been crushed by it. Now she could see that it was as automatic for him to hold people at arm's length as it was for her to embrace them. Couldn't he see how that made them perfect for each other? He could teach her caution. She could teach him to love.

First, though, she had to get him to stop rescuing her. Sam needed an equal, a woman who wouldn't be dependent on him for anything except his love. She could see that now. He feared anyone needing him too much, because as Dana had reminded her, all he had known in his life was abandonment. He obviously figured he was destined to repeat the pattern, hurting any woman who dared to love him or being hurt by anyone he risked loving.

But how did she go about showing him that she was strong enough to survive on her own without making it seem that there was no place for him in her life? For all of her education, she wasn't smart enough to figure that out. It was a balance that had stymied men and women for eons.

Disgusted by her inability to get to sleep or to solve her dilemma about Sam, she reached for one of the books by her bed. Chaucer. In Old English. That ought to test her powers of concentration. There'd be no room in her brain at all for wayward thoughts of the man who might at this very moment be sleeping stark naked on her living room sofa. Oh, Lordy, what an image!

Warm milk, she decided. Wasn't that what everyone recommended for times like this? Unfortunately, the potentially naked Sam was between her and the kitchen. She decided it didn't matter. He was probably sleeping by now. He probably hadn't wasted a single second tormented by thoughts of her before drifting off. Typical!

She tiptoed to the bedroom door and peeked out. The living room was bathed in shadows, the only light coming from the streetlight outside. Sam was on the sofa, tangled in sheets, his feet poking over the end. She felt a momentary twinge of guilt at having relegated him to such an uncomfortable bed. Not that it seemed to have bothered him. She could hear the faint, steady whisper of his breathing. Sound asleep, damn him!

She crept closer, swearing to herself that she wasn't trying to sneak a look at any bare parts that might be showing. She would just straighten the sheet a little, cover his . . . well, whatever needed to be covered.

Unfortunately, Sam in repose was no less sexy than he was wide awake. His hair was tousled, his cheeks shadowed by the faint beginning of a beard, his chest matted with golden hairs that arrowed down, drawing her gaze lower, and lower. She swallowed hard as he shifted slightly, sending the sheet in a slow, provocative slide toward the floor.

Dear heaven, he wasn't swearing a stitch. Her pulse bucked. She tried to make herself back away. She really did. But she felt as if she'd been frozen in place. Bad choice of words. If she'd been frozen, the heated thoughts tumbling through her mind would have defrosted her in a split second. She was . . . fascinated, awestruck, *hot*.

And caught. While she was absorbed in examining his body with the exquisite attention to detail of an artist in a life-drawing class, he reached out and snared her wrist. The movement was so quick, so unexpected, that Penny yelped in shock.

"I thought you were asleep," she said accusingly.

"I know," he said.

He spoke in that smug, lazy, smoky voice that twisted her insides into a knot. She couldn't see his face, wouldn't even look at his face, but she could just imagine the grin. She tried to wrench free, but his grip was like steel.

"Let go of me," she demanded. "And put some clothes on."

He actually chuckled at that. "Hey, I was sleeping in this miserable bed you consigned me to, when you came in here to spy on me. It's not my fault you got an eyeful."

She noticed he didn't even reach for the sheet. "I wasn't spying. I came out to get some warm milk."

"The kitchen's that way," he pointed out.

"A gentleman wouldn't humiliate me like this."

"I'm no gentleman," he reminded her, apparently taking some pride in the fact. "And you may be slightly embarrassed, but you're not humiliated. You're probably just sorry you got caught before you'd seen everything. Go ahead, look to your heart's content. I'm willing."

"Oh, go to hell," she muttered, and this time when she tried to pull free he let her go. Head held high, she stalked off to the kitchen. She doubted the exit was nearly as dignified as she might have liked.

Penny flipped on the kitchen light and opened the refrigerator, then realized she was not alone. Daring a glance to see what Sam was wearing, if anything, she was relieved to discover that he'd knotted the sheet around his waist. It left his chest bare and rode dangerously low on his hips, but for the moment, he was decent. At least as decent as he was probably inclined to get. He probably fully intended to torment her. In fact, if that sparkle of amusement in his eyes was anything to judge by, he was enjoying this moment quite a bit more than many others they had shared.

"Warm milk?" she offered casually, even though her heart was pounding as if she'd raced to the corner convenience store and back to pick up the quart container she held in her hand.

He shook his head. "I'm just here to keep you company."

"It's not necessary."

"I know. It's my pleasure."

"I'll just bet," she muttered under her breath as she slammed a saucepan onto the stove and turned on the heat.

"You'd better lower the flame, sweetheart, or you'll scald it."

"I know what I'm doing," she snapped, but she lowered the flame, then sloshed half the quart of milk into the pan.

"Whiskey'd probably work better," Sam suggested.

She scowled at him. "Would you like a drink?"

He shook his head. "I'm not the one having trouble sleeping." Suddenly his expression sobered. "You weren't having nightmares, were you?"

"No."

"He won't get to you, Penny. I promise," he said, obviously mistaking the cause of her distress.

Her hand shook as she tried to pour the milk into a cup. Milk splattered all over the counter. Sam was up in a heartbeat, taking the pan, filling the cup and handing it to her, then mopping up the spill. Penny sank onto a chair and stared miserably at the milk. She tasted it and made a face.

"Something wrong?" he inquired.

"It's awful. Why would anybody recommend this?"

Sam reached for the bottle of whiskey on the counter and poured in a shot. "Try it now."

She took another sip. It didn't taste any better but it warmed her all the way to her toes. After the third sip, she began to relax. "Not bad," she said, barely stifling a yawn. She stretched.

Sam grinned at her. "Why do I have the feeling if you finish that whole cup, I'm going to be carrying you back to bed?"

"An interesting thought," she admitted sleepily, and took a long swallow of the disgusting stuff.

"Hey, you had your chance. You turned me down."

Penny let the taunt pass. She suddenly felt incredibly groggy. No doubt that's what happened when adrenaline wore off and whiskey took effect. She reminded herself to beware of that particular combination in the future. Right now, though, it was all she could do to hold her head up.

"I think I can sleep now," she said. She stood and wobbled.

"First you have to get back to bed," Sam noted, scooping her up before she could protest.

She curved her arms around his neck and snuggled against his bare chest. He was warm and strong, and if she had just the tiniest bit more energy, she might very well try to take advantage of him, she decided.

As it was, she barely managed to plant a kiss of gratitude somewhere on his shoulder. It felt so good, she snuck in one more on his neck. She thought she heard him groan, but before she could figure out why, she sighed and drifted off to sleep.

Sam's entire body, head to toe and especially in between, ached with longing. It had been a mistake picking Penny up in the kitchen. He should have forced her to walk to the bedroom under her own steam. The gallant gesture had turned out to be the sweetest torment of his entire life. The woman cuddled like a friendly kitten.

He stood beside her bed even now that she was sound asleep in his arms. He was unable to overcome his reluctance to put her down. There was something so trusting in the way she'd twined her arms around his neck, so innocently sensual in the kisses she'd bestowed. She felt right in his arms, as if she belonged there. The temptation to believe that taunted him.

Unfortunately, if he didn't put her into the bed and under the covers very quickly, he was not going to be responsible for his actions. From the moment he'd awakened to find her standing over him, her fascinated gaze locked on his all-too-responsive body, he'd been fighting a battle with temptation. He had mistakenly figured that getting her out of that living room untouched meant he had won the battle.

He waged one more war with himself and managed to emerge on the side of the saints. He lowered her to the bed, pulled the sheet up over her and counted himself lucky. Another victory.

But he couldn't seem to make himself walk out the door. He debated a long time over it, too. He gave himself at least a dozen logical, moralistic reasons for getting the hell out of her bedroom, topped by the fact that things between them had gone too far already.

He had only one reason for staying: she might have a nightmare. He figured that outweighed all the others in favor of leaving. He also figured he was lying to himself if he believed that was the only reason he was stretching out beside her, albeit on top of the covers, arms over his head, hands dutifully linked behind his neck.

Now he was the one who couldn't sleep. Every square inch of him fairly hummed with awareness of the woman beside him. He decided if he made it until morning without losing his mind or doing something they'd both regret, he would reward himself by taking the day off, going fishing, taking a drive in the country, anything to put several hours and a lot of miles between him and Penny.

That vow did not take into account that Penny was a restless sleeper. When she rolled onto her side and flung her arm across his chest, Sam sucked in his breath and counted to ten.

When she snuggled into his side and used his shoulder for a pillow, he groaned and counted to a hundred, very rapidly. When that didn't help, he started over and slowly and determinedly counted to a thousand.

When she shifted again and slid her bare thigh across his, his willpower snapped. Even with that thin, cotton sheet between them, he could feel her heat. His body responded as if they'd skipped foreplay and gone straight to the peak of lovemaking. He was throbbing with the desperate need for more intimate contact. He wanted to fill her, to feel her moving in response to the urgent rhythm he set. He'd played with fire by getting into this bed, no matter what his motives had been.

And he'd lost. He wanted her so badly his teeth ached. He might as well admit that she'd gotten under his skin. But what would he do about it? Making love to her while she was sound asleep was not one of the options, he told himself sternly. He wanted her awake and willing. Unfortunately, he knew in his gut that it wouldn't be all that difficult to make that happen.

Drawing on one last shred of decency, he made himself concentrate on taming the pace of his heart. Relaxation therapy, that was the ticket out of this fix. Maybe those stress reduction classes he'd been forced to take would pay off, after all. He deliberately slowed his breathing. With one arm, he settled Penny more comfortably—and less provocatively—in his embrace. With the other he smoothed the tangle of hair from her face. His fingers lingered on her cheek. It was as soft as he'd remembered and flushed from resting against his shoulder.

She sighed contentedly.

So far, so good, he told himself. She was sound asleep. He'd tamed the immediate need to seduce her. He glanced at the clock. It was 3:00 a.m. Penny had set her alarm for six. Only three more hours of this torture.

It was only later, when she was wide awake, thoroughly indignant and warm as sin in his arms, that he wondered why the hell he hadn't gotten out of her bed when he'd had the chance.

Wedged between Sam and the wall, Penny scrambled out of Sam's arms and onto her knees on the bed. She yanked the sheet up to her chin even though she was wearing perfectly respectable pajamas, then glared down into Sam's amused expression.

"What the hell are you doing in my bed?" she demanded, not pausing to consider the fact that a couple of days ago this was precisely where she'd wanted him.

His eyes glinted with barely contained laughter. "Isn't that what the three bears asked Goldilocks?"

She scowled at him. "I'm not up on my nursery rhymes. I'd prefer to deal with your presence, your *uninvited* presence, in my bed."

"Do you recall my crawling between the sheets with you?"

"No. Absolutely not."

"Then how can you be sure you didn't invite me?"

"Because I would never, not in a million years, have done that," she said staunchly, despite the fact that a little voice in her head was screaming *liar* at the top of its lungs.

"You're sure, absolutely sure?" he asked, his expression all innocent puzzlement.

"Sam Roberts, I am not in the habit of inviting anyone into my bed."

"Oh, really? I'm delighted to hear it."

She eyed him warily, wondering at the genuine note of pleasure she'd heard in his voice. What did that mean? Probably nothing, she decided.

Penny wanted badly to cut her losses, but she couldn't quite figure out how a lady went about exiting a bed with a very attractive, very sexy man in it, especially when she very much wanted to fling herself on top of him. She considered telling him to leave, but the memory of his lack of clothing stopped her. Telling a naked man to parade across the room was more than she could cope with at 6:00 a.m.

So, it was up to her. Dragging the sheet with her, she stood and stepped over him with as much grace as she could muster, then hopped off the bed onto the floor.

"I hope when I get out of the shower, you will have the decency to be up and dressed," she said without looking at him.

"What about my shower?"

She knew where he was heading with the question from the suggestive tone of his voice. She tried to cut him off. "Take one at home."

"No time. I could join you," he offered cheerfully.

She whirled on him. "You're enjoying this, aren't you?"

"Not half as much as I was enjoying having you cuddled up next to me."

A vague memory of snuggling up to something warm made Penny's face burn with embarrassment. And his arms had been around her when she'd awakened. How they'd gotten there was irrelevant. A denial appeared to be pointless. She just shot him what she hoped was a withering look, walked into the bathroom and slammed the door. And locked it. She didn't trust him a bit when he was in this kind of provocative mood. Only when she figured she was safe did she allow herself to smile.

Things were definitely heating up, whether Sam wanted them to or not. She figured it was only a short leap from sleeping together in the traditional sense to *sleeping together* in the euphemistic, sexual connotation of the phrase.

She could hardly wait.

Chapter Ten

"So there I was, pinned between him and the wall, and he wasn't wearing a stitch of clothing," Penny told Didi later that morning during a coffee break. She still hadn't entirely come to grips with everything that had gone on the night before. Something told her that Didi would be able to give her a wiser, more experienced and definitely more objective view of the amazing events.

"And you got out of the bed," her friend said, her expression registering total disbelief.

"Of course I got out of there."

"Why?"

Why, indeed, Penny thought to herself. "Because

he would have hated me if I'd stayed and he would have hated himself even more.''

Didi waved off the explanation. "The man is nuts about you. He didn't show up at that diner last night out of a sense of obligation. He was clearly terrified that something might happen to you.''

"Sure," Penny agreed. "And he would have blamed himself. That's all.''

Didi rolled her eyes. "Oh, please. Will you wake up and smell the coffee?'' She waved her cup under Penny's nose for emphasis. "Don't you ever look into the man's eyes?''

"Yes.''

"Well? What do you see?''

"I see a man who's fighting his own instincts.''

"Exactly," Didi said triumphantly as if an inept pupil had finally grasped an important point. "And why do you think he's doing that?''

"Because he wants me.''

"Bravo!''

"But he doesn't want to want me," Penny reminded her. "You've spent enough time around him. He's the most stubborn man on the face of the earth. Do you honestly think he ever does anything he doesn't want to do?''

"Oh, I'd say he's on the edge right about now. Do you think he crawled into your bed last night to keep you from rolling out?''

Penny chuckled despite herself. "No, I suppose not.''

"I know not. All you need to do is turn up the heat another notch and he will be powerless to resist."

Penny doubted her ability to overcome Sam's resistance under any conditions, but even she had to admit that she'd seen definite signs that he was wavering. But when the mighty fell, did they go graciously or did they wind up resenting the very person who'd brought about their downfall?

For a solid week Sam worried about the lighthearted enjoyment he'd gotten from tormenting Penny about their sleeping arrangements. That worry had brought him to Johnny's Place night after night, hoping that a workout with the punching bag and a few rounds in the ring would drive the memories from his head. It hadn't worked. Even so, he was back at it again tonight, sure that this time would succeed in accomplishing what all the other times had not.

Sweat poured down his chest. His arms ached from pummeling the bag, but still the images were there. He'd liked watching the pink tint flood into Penny's cheeks. He'd thrilled to the fire of indignation sparkling in her eyes. Most of all, he'd taken a definite masculine pride in seeing her respond to him and believing with everything in him that he was the first to affect her that way.

Some people would have told him it was just a typical macho reaction and maybe it was. But he had the disturbing feeling there was more to it. This had been Penny, not just any woman he'd asked out on a casual date. Hell, with most women he didn't waste time

156 A VOW TO LOVE

on all the preliminary flirting. The women he chose were more than willing to accept the casual status of a relationship with him and leave it at that. They knew the rules and found them satisfactory.

With Penny, all of his carefully crafted rules had flown out the window. Some of that had to do with her ties to Brandon Halloran. Her grandfather would personally escort Sam to an abandoned island and leave him there if he hurt Penny, if he used her and abandoned her.

Most of his reaction, however, had to do with the woman herself. She had admitted that she didn't indulge in casual affairs. In fact, if he had to hazard a guess, she hadn't indulged in any affairs whatsoever. Sam found that to be both a blessing and a curse. The thought of her with any other man made his stomach twist into knots. He was almost irrationally relieved to know it was something he didn't need to think about. And yet...

And yet, things would have been a helluva lot simpler if she'd been like every other worldly woman he'd been attracted to. Virginity was a definite complication for a man who craved simplicity. Women, especially women Penny's age, who'd waited all their lives for the right man, were very dangerous to a man who didn't want to be anybody's destiny.

Just the thought of entanglement in a relationship made him slam his fists into the punching bag with a force that jarred him. His breath was coming in pants as he took out his frustrations on that inanimate object.

"I—" He slammed a right cross into the bag.

"Will—" He jabbed with his left.

"Not—" He aimed a right about chin high into the bag.

"Get—" An uppercut with his left rocked him on his heels.

"Involved!" He delivered a knockout punch with his right.

"Hey, Sam, who're you talking to?" Randy asked, watching him with a puzzled expression.

"Myself," he admitted. "Take it from me. Wait until you're at least forty before you start to date."

Randy grinned at him, his expression all too knowing. "Ms. Hayden giving you trouble?"

Sam scowled at him. "Ms. Hayden has nothing to do with this. What gave you that idea?"

"She's been talking to herself a lot this week, too."

Small comfort, Sam thought. "You seeing a lot of her?"

"Just what we talked about. I walk her to work in the morning and meet her at night. She's a terrific lady. Did you know she's got an undergraduate degree in microbiology and is getting her Ph.D. in English?"

Sam personally thought that was a sign of a woman who couldn't make up her mind what she wanted to be when she grew up. Randy obviously thought otherwise. In fact, he was showing all the signs of developing a full-fledged crush on the lady. He'd even started letting his hair grow into a more traditional style.

"She says she'll tutor me to get my high school diploma and then help me apply to colleges."

Sam stared at him in amazement. Randy had never before expressed the slightest desire to further his education. Apparently working miracles was another of Penny's hidden talents.

"That's great," he said carefully. "What do you want to study?"

Randy suddenly looked downright shy. "Criminal justice," he admitted, his gaze fixed on Sam for approval. "I want to be a cop, so I can help kids like you do."

To his astonishment, Sam felt the sting of what might have been tears in his eyes. The kid was finally on the right track and for the first time after months of worry, Sam was certain Randy would make it. Oh, he had his reservations about police officers who spent years learning theory before they discovered the realities of the streets, but Randy knew all too much about the streets. He'd do just fine with or without college. If Penny had talked him into higher education, Sam didn't want to discourage him in any way. And he couldn't ignore the signs of hero worship written plainly on the teen's face.

"You need any extra help, you let me know," he said, his voice gruff with an emotion he couldn't express. "And when the time comes to get on the force, I'll see what I can do."

Randy grinned. "Ms. Hayden already told me you would."

Sam laughed. "Oh, she did, did she?"

"I think she's really got it bad for you."

Worry warred with pleasure. Pleasure won by a hairsbreadth. "Oh?" he said, even though he thought a man had to be pretty pitiful to be pumping a sixteen-year-old for information about a woman.

"She asks about you all the time. I guess that means you haven't seen her lately."

"Not for the last few days, anyway."

"How come?"

"I've been busy."

"Don't wait too long," Randy warned. "There's this guy from the lab. I think he's got the hots for her. He's been hanging around a lot."

Sam hit the punching bag so hard, it jarred his teeth. He would not, he absolutely would not, ask about the man. It was her life. She could date anyone she wanted. In fact, that's what he'd been hoping for, right? To be let off the hook?

"Who is he?" he demanded.

Randy grinned at him. "Nobody, man. I just wanted to be sure I had things pegged right."

Sam chuckled despite himself. "Go get ready, kid. And you'd better be on your toes in that ring, because I am out to get you."

They went five rounds with Randy holding his own before the teen looked up at the clock and called a halt. "I've got to get to the lab. Ms. Hayden will be off soon."

Sam made a split-second decision. "Take the night off. I'll meet her."

Randy shot him a man-to-man grin. "I think she'll be real glad to see you."

That was a slight overstatement, Sam discovered as he watched Penny pick him out of the cluster of people lingering on the sidewalk outside of the lab. She lifted her hand in a halfhearted wave, but her expression was nervous.

"Where's Randy?" she asked when she'd joined him.

"Hi, Sam. Thanks for coming, Sam. I've missed you, Sam," he prompted, and saw a smile tug at her lips.

"Hi, Sam," she began, but left it at that.

"Hi, short stuff. I gave Randy the night off. I thought we'd go to Rosie's."

"Did I hear an invitation in there somewhere?"

He grinned. "Would you like to go to Rosie's?"

She grinned back at him. "I would love to. But let me warn you, I'm starved. I never got out of the lab for lunch today."

"Given Rosie's prices, I doubt you're going to break me. If you do, she'll probably extend me credit."

"Based on your good looks and personality, no doubt."

"Based on the tab she's been running for me ever since I've known her. She keeps hoping maybe someday I'll hit a lottery and turn most of it over to her."

Rosie welcomed them with exuberant hugs and chastized them for staying away so long. Penny turned a commiserating look on Sam.

"I was here last week. How about you?"

"Two nights ago."

Rosie wasn't fazed. "You should come every night, like it was your mama's table. Sit and I'll bring you wine."

While Rosie fussed over them, Sam studied Penny. "You're still not sleeping, are you?" he asked eventually.

"Why do you say that?"

"Those dark circles under your eyes don't look like the latest style in makeup. You worried about Tank?" He regarded her slyly. "Or are you missing me?"

"You? I haven't given you a thought," she said, but not very convincingly. "I've been studying late and getting up early for work."

Sam let the explanation pass. It might have been the truth, though he doubted it. She'd seemed too flustered by his questions. "Are you sure this schedule isn't too much for you?"

"It'll be better next session. I have independent study. I can work my reading in around work a little better."

"Why do you want this degree? From what I hear, English degrees aren't exactly in huge demand in the marketplace."

"I might want to teach someday. Or maybe write. I think I have a book locked away inside me. I intend to try to write it for my thesis."

"Then why on earth did you start out in microbiology?"

"It's fascinating stuff. Besides, maybe I can make a contribution to humanity, discover something really important."

"Doesn't it strike you that you'd probably accomplish more if you picked one or the other and really concentrated on it?"

Penny regarded Sam evenly, clearly not the least bit offended by the criticism. He guessed she'd had to undergo the same cross-examination by any number of family members already. She'd probably had to fight off Brandon's attempts to get her into the family business, just as he had. He knew the kind of will it took to withstand Brandon's persuasiveness.

"I do give them everything I've got," she informed him. "When I'm in the lab, I'm totally focused. When I read or write, I'm totally absorbed in that. Maybe it will take me a little longer to make great accomplishments in one or the other because I'm dividing my time, but what's the rush? If it takes both for me to feel fulfilled, then that's the way I have to go."

"Doesn't seem as if it would leave much time for a personal life."

She shrugged. "I don't have one."

"By choice?"

"Because there aren't a lot of men who fascinate me as much as my work does."

"Present company included?"

She evaded his eyes at that.

"Penny?"

She lifted her gaze finally. "My impression was that present company wasn't interested in my social life, except from a distant, analytical point of view."

He winced. "I can think of at least two recent occasions when I've demonstrated otherwise."

"A few kisses? Sneaking into my bed? I chalked those off as experiments which resulted in insufficient evidence from which to draw a conclusion."

He grinned. "Are you angling for more experiments?"

"I wouldn't want you to put yourself out."

"Oh, I think I can probably manage to survive a few hours in your company."

"Thank you so very much."

"Penny?"

"Hmm?"

"You realize this is a very dangerous gamble, don't you?"

She leveled a mischievous look at him. "For you or me?"

"I'd say we both have a lot to lose."

"And even more to gain," she retorted softly.

Sam was so busy replaying her taunting words in his mind as he walked back to his car later that night that he missed the approach of the five young men who came out of the shadows to surround him. Tank waved a knife in his face.

"I guess we'll find out who the tough guy is now," the teenager taunted.

"You don't want to do this," Sam said quietly. "Assaulting a police officer carries a very stiff penalty."

"If he lives to tell who did it," Tank retorted smugly. "I'd say the odds are in my favor at the moment."

"Is that how you intend to prove to your friends here how tough you are? It's an uneven fight. You've got a weapon. I don't. Drop the knife and we'll see who wins in a fair fight."

"I ain't interested in fair, man. I'm looking to get even for every time you've busted my chops, every time you've looked down your nose at me. I'm going to carve up that pretty face of yours and then you can see if your lady friend will take a second look at you."

Without further warning, he slashed the knife through the air. Sam ducked instinctively and saw the blur as it barely missed his cheek. He felt the sting as it nicked his shoulder instead. Tank's next slice was poorly aimed and gave Sam a chance to grab his arm and twist it. He kneed him in the groin and heard his grunt of pain.

"Get him," Tank ordered, sounding breathless and furious.

Sam could have taken on two of them, maybe even three, but not five. They closed in around him, pinning him in place for Tank's attack.

Sam tried to get to the gun he had tucked into his boot, the one he'd sworn he didn't have and didn't want to use, but one of the boys slammed a punch into his midsection and doubled him over. Gagging and trying to catch his breath, he again reached for the gun, only to have Tank stab him again...and again. The pain was unbearable and unrelenting and then it faded as the world turned hazy and distant. He was losing blood.

It was the distant sound of sirens that probably saved him.

"Cops!" one of the teens warned, and then they were all gone, leaving him in an agony of pain, crumpled on the sidewalk in a pool of his own blood.

Just before he passed out, Sam thought he heard Penny's voice calling to him, demanding that he hold on. He could have sworn he felt her hand caressing his cheek, felt the brush of her lips across his, but that couldn't be. She was inside her apartment half a block away, safe. Dammit, she had to be safe.

Chapter Eleven

Penny stood by the pay phone in the emergency room shaking uncontrollably as she fumbled with her address book and tried to dial Dana's unfamiliar number. She got two wrong numbers, awakening some very cranky strangers, before she finally got it right by hitting the numbers with careful deliberation. As it rang, she tried to think of what she would say to Sam's sister.

Even though the paramedics in the ambulance had promised her that Sam was going to make it, she hadn't believed them. He'd been so terribly pale and his hand in hers had been like ice. She'd wanted to throw herself onto the stretcher to warm him. Only the awareness that the paramedics were providing him with essential treatments had kept her from shoving them aside to take over his care herself.

When Jason finally answered the phone, his voice groggy with sleep, it was all Penny could do to keep from sobbing. "Jason?"

"Yes. Who is this?"

"It's Penny. Penny Hayden."

"Are you okay?" he asked, instantly picking up on the alarm in her voice.

"It's not me. It's Sam," she said, choking back a note of hysteria. "He's in surgery."

"An accident?"

"No. He was attacked outside my apartment. I think it was one of those gangs."

"How bad is it?" he asked.

The calm note in his voice soothed her. She could hear Dana asking questions in the background. Penny wanted to reassure her, to reassure herself, but she couldn't find the words. "The paramedics said he would make it, but I'm scared," she admitted. "He lost so much blood."

"We'll be there as soon as we can find someone to look after the kids," he promised. "Hold on, okay?"

"I'm trying."

Penny retreated to the waiting room and huddled in a chair, trying to ward off the chill of stark terror. She couldn't lose him, not like this. Not now. The moment she had seen him on the street, lying there bleeding and unconscious, she had realized with absolute clarity that what she'd dismissed all these years as a silly infatuation really was love, a love that had been tested by time—for her, anyway.

She was hardly aware of the passing of time, but a nurse brought her a cup of coffee and promised to return when there was any news from the operating room. It seemed like forever, but it was probably no more than an hour before Jason and Dana arrived. Dana's eyes widened in horror at the sight of all the blood spattered on Penny's clothes.

"Oh, my God, were you hurt, too?" she asked, dropping into the chair beside Penny and enfolding Penny's hands in her own warmer, stronger grasp.

"No, I wasn't there. He'd just dropped me off," she said in a shaky voice. "It happened as he was going back to his car. Randy, this kid who's been keeping an eye on me for Sam, saw the guys come out of an alley. Thank goodness he was there. Sam had given him the night off, but Randy took his assignment seriously. He passed by just to check things out. Anyway, when he saw what was happening, he ran to my apartment and I called for help. By the time I got downstairs, the ambulance was on its way and the gang had taken off."

Dana looked puzzled. "Why was somebody watching you?"

"It's a long story, but a gang leader had threatened me. Sam's been trying to keep an eye on me. When he wasn't available, Randy took over."

Tears welled up in Dana's eyes before she turned away from Penny. She stood and began to pace.

"I knew it," she said, her gaze going to her husband. "I knew one of these days he was going to get hurt. I hate the fact that he's a cop. When this is over, I'm going to insist that he leave the force."

Jason pulled her into his arms. "No, you're not. You know this is something he has to do. Being a cop is who he is."

"Well, he can damned well be something else," Dana snapped angrily.

Penny could sympathize. In the past hour she'd grown to despise the job that put Sam's life in danger every single day. Chances were when things calmed down, Dana wouldn't say a word to him, but Penny vowed that she would. She would not have him endangering his life just because he thought he didn't matter to anyone. With a sudden flash of insight, she realized that that conviction was behind all of his actions. Couldn't he see how many people cared about him? Hadn't he figured out yet how much his life was worth?

Just look at the gathering in the waiting room. In the time since word had gone out about the attack, Ryan and Jake had turned up, along with several other police officers. Dana and Jason had been joined by Kevin and Lacey. And Randy hovered nearby. Penny went to him.

"Would you like to go to the chapel with me?"

He lifted his distressed face and met her gaze. Finally he nodded. "I haven't said too many prayers in my life," he admitted.

She squeezed his hand. "Then this one will count even more," she promised.

They sat side by side in the dimly lit hospital chapel for what seemed an eternity. They were still there when Jason came in search of them.

"He's out of surgery."

Penny waited for more.

Jason smiled at her. "The doctors say he'll be fine."

An astonishing sense of relief washed through her. He would be fine, she repeated to herself. And then she vowed to strangle him herself if he ever took unnecessary chances again.

"You're very lucky," the doctor said to Sam a few hours after he finally regained consciousness.

They'd told him it had taken forty-eight hours for him to emerge from the haze of painkillers and anesthetic. He'd come to and started yelling. He'd raised such a ruckus that the nurses had fled, sending Dr. Kline to settle him down. Apparently the physician's favorite technique for taming a troublesome patient was to scare him to death.

"A hairsbreadth to the right and he'd have cut a main artery," the surgeon added. "You would not be in here giving all my nurses a rough time. You'd be on a slab at the morgue. As it is, you should come away from this with nothing more than a nasty scar or two. Most of your wounds were superficial."

"How comforting."

"Don't knock it. It will impress the hell out of the ladies. One in particular has been fascinated with the damage ever since we brought you in."

He dragged his head off the pillow. "Penny? Where is she?" Awakening alone, he had been struck anew by the fear that she had been harmed in the attack.

"Not to worry," Dr. Kline soothed, his manner changing in response to Sam's obvious distress. "I sent her off for coffee. I would have preferred she go home and get some sleep, but she hasn't budged any farther than the hospital cafeteria."

So she had been there, Sam thought. "Was she hurt?"

"No. You can stop your worrying on that score. From what I hear she arrived at the same time as the ambulance, insisted on coming along for the ride. She has a stubborn streak a lot like yours."

"Who called for help?"

The doctor shook his head. "She'll have to tell you that. My expertise begins with your arrival on our doorstep."

"I want out."

The doctor grinned. "I'll just bet you do."

"Well?"

"Not if you threatened me with jail time." He waved on his way out.

For the next hour there was a steady parade of visitors beginning with Dana and Jason and Kevin and Lacey, all offering him a place to stay when he was eventually released. He responded testily to the of-

fers. Then Ryan and Jake stopped by with a promise
to have Tank and his pals locked up before the end of
the day. They vowed to see that they were tried as
adults and spent a long, long time in prison. Sam reacted crankily to them, as well, his eyes peeled on the
door, waiting for Penny to return. He wanted to see
for himself that Tank hadn't gotten to her. Fear
warred with impatience.

When Penny eventually sashayed into his room, he
took out his frustration on her before he noted the
exhaustion on her face and the blood spatters all over
her clothes. She hadn't even taken time to go home
and change clothes. Alarm at her appearance made
him even more irritable.

"What are you doing here?" he demanded. "You
should be at home getting some rest."

"Rumor has it some creep tried to cut you down to
size," she said, reacting to his testiness with amazing
calm. "I thought I'd stick around to hear your version."

"It wouldn't have happened if there hadn't been
five of them," he grumbled. "I couldn't keep my eyes
on all of them at once."

"Tank, I assume. At least, that's what Randy
thought. He saved your life, you know. He ran to my
apartment and we called for help. Whoever attacked
you had run off by the time we got back outside."

"It was Tank."

"How come you didn't spot him?"

"My mind was on other things," he admitted reluctantly, recalling the conversation they'd had only

moments before the attack. "It'll never happen again."

"Too bad he didn't aim for your hard head. The knife would probably have ricocheted off."

This wasn't going the way he'd meant it to at all. He'd expected a woman who'd spent two days at his bedside to display a little sympathy. She wasn't giving him an inch. "Did you stick around here to cheer me up?" he asked.

"Sure did."

"You're doing a lousy job of it."

"Ah, but I have news. Word is that you want out."

"I asked. The doctor said no."

"Obviously you didn't use your charm on him. He told me he would be willing to spring you day after tomorrow if you will go someplace where someone can watch out for you and where you will be guaranteed a week or so of bedrest."

"I can watch out for myself."

She glared at him with obvious impatience. "Do you want to get out of here or not? The entire medical complex has voted you worst patient of the year and you've only been awake for the past couple of hours. When Didi calls because she's heard the grumbling clear over in the labs, it has to be bad. Pretty soon, they're liable to start withholding food just to weaken your spirit."

"So what the hell am I supposed to do? Hire a baby-sitter?

Wide blue eyes regarded him thoughtfully. "Let's see now. You could have gone to Jason and Dana's, but you turned them down. As I recall, you said something about not being cooped up with a squalling brat, one neurotic toddler and a budding delinquent, which I might add would probably earn you ten to twenty in prison if Grandfather heard you talking that way about his great-grandchildren."

He flinched. "Dana knew I didn't mean it. They're actually great kids."

"Perhaps you'll tell them how great they are, if Dana and Jason ever permit you near them again. Now let me think. Kevin and Lacey were willing to have you stay out at Cape Cod, but what were your exact words?"

She regarded him expectantly. He remained stubbornly, guiltily silent. It didn't matter. She filled them in for him. "I believe you told them if you wanted to retire to the damned beach, you'd go someplace that wasn't overrun with tourists. Was that it?"

"Something like that," he muttered. "So what's your point?"

She studied him with a look that made him very, very wary.

"Looks like I'm elected," she announced.

"You?" he repeated weakly. This was beginning to sound like a very bad idea. Perhaps he should just stay put and deal with the whims of the nurses.

"That's right. Me. Grandfather's already called from California to check on you. He says we can stay over at his place."

"What's wrong with my own apartment? I'd rather be in my own place."

"Yeah, well, we don't always get what we want in life. Besides, do you honestly think the two of us could survive without killing each other in that cramped space you've described to me? Ditto my apartment. Besides, the housekeeper's at Grandfather's."

Sam sensed a new twist in Brandon's plot. Even though he might have wanted something exactly like this, he reacted with suspicion now that Brandon's fine hand was involved. "If Mrs. Farnsworth is around, why do I need you?" he inquired testily.

"To keep her from quitting," she said succinctly.

Chapter Twelve

It was just for a couple of days, a week at the out-side, Penny told herself the next night as she packed a bag to take across town in the morning. She could put up with anything, even a foul-tempered beast like Sam Roberts, for that long. Who knew, maybe she'd even become totally disenchanted with the man. That would be a welcome change from the anguish she'd felt when a nearly incoherent Randy had come pounding into her apartment, tears streaming down his face while she frantically dialed 9-1-1.

She had relived the terror of the next few hours over and over again in her mind. In the time it had taken her to figure out what had happened to Sam and to reach him where he lay bleeding on the sidewalk, she had died a thousand deaths.

Ironically, her distress had calmed Randy and he'd knelt beside her, reassuring her over and over that Sam would be all right. He'd demonstrated a maturity far beyond his years and she'd been grateful for his presence in the emergency room while she and the rest of the family had awaited word on Sam's fate.

In the middle of the night when the trauma surgeon had eventually made the same promise for his recovery that she'd heard from the paramedics, she hadn't entirely believed it. Only when Sam had regained consciousness the previous afternoon had she finally been convinced.

Then, when she'd returned to Sam's room and been the target of his cranky attitude, she had known he was already on the road to recovery. Relief had washed through her even as he'd verbally sparred with her. She'd thought then that she would take endless doses of his foul humor any day over losing him. She'd actually looked forward to the coming days together.

Twenty-four hours later, after they'd settled into Brandon's, Penny wasn't so sure either of them would survive Sam's slow recovery process. She was beginning to understand why the hospital had been so anxious to get rid of him. Saying that Sam was a bad patient was like saying Attila the Hun had a minor interest in power. His shouts echoed through her grandfather's house.

"Dammit, get your hands off of me! Penny! Penny!"

Sitting at the kitchen table having a much needed cup of tea, Penny glanced at Mrs. Farnsworth, whose expression was filled with tolerant amusement.

"I guess he doesn't care to be bathed by the visiting nurse's aide," Penny noted dryly.

"He'd probably rather it be you," the housekeeper said, looking innocent as a lamb as Penny choked on her tea.

Penny doubted it was anything that lascivious. He was just being obstinate and mule-headed. "Is it time for his painkiller yet?" she inquired hopefully. "That usually knocks him out for an hour or so."

Mrs. Farnsworth grinned. "He just took it. Probably stuck it under his pillow, if I know him."

"Was he this obnoxious as a teenager?"

"Worse. And he wasn't even sick when he'd hang around here then."

Penny shook her head. "Hard to believe Grandfather didn't beat the dickens out of him."

"Are you kidding? Those two were thick as thieves from the minute they met. Mr. Halloran always did admire a person with spunk. He loved having Sammy drop by."

"Then Mr. Halloran ought to be back here babysitting him."

Any further observations about the patient's temperament were cut short by another indignant shout. "Hell, woman, what are you trying to do? Scrub the skin off me? Penny! Get up here!"

Penny and the housekeeper exchanged a glance.

"I guess I'd better get upstairs before the woman refuses to set foot inside the house again," Penny said. "Have you got some lemonade? That ought to suit his sour mood."

"Just made a fresh pitcher. You go on up. I'll bring it."

Penny reluctantly climbed the stairs. The nurse, an expression of grim satisfaction on her face, met her halfway up.

"Everything okay?" Penny asked Ruth Dawkins, a handsome African-American woman with twenty years experience dealing with surly patients. She didn't look any the worse for her encounter with Sam.

"It is now," she said. "Showed him this great big needle in my bag and told him I'd use it to dose him up with tranquilizers, if he didn't mind his manners."

Penny didn't even try to contain her grin. "How'd he react?"

"He's quiet, isn't he? I'll be back tomorrow. Same time. I don't expect I'll be having any more trouble."

"No, I don't expect you will," Penny said. "Thanks, Ruth."

"Honey, you decide to marry that man, I'd suggest you have counseling first to talk you out of it. He's a fine-looking man, but he's got the temper of the devil."

"I don't think marriage is an issue, but if it ever comes up, I'll remember your advice. Maybe I'll even borrow that needle of yours."

She climbed the remaining stairs quickly. She wanted to see if Ruth had actually tamed the beast. She found him sprawled across clean sheets, his head propped up against freshly fluffed pillows. His blond hair was tousled and he was still unshaven. Apparently he'd refused to allow Mrs. Dawkins near him with a razor or comb.

The top sheet was draped strategically, leaving his bandaged chest bare and one leg poking out. Penny seriously doubted Ruth had left him covered so provocatively. She'd probably tucked that sheet up to his handsome chin.

He turned an accusing look on Penny. "You left me alone with a crazy woman."

"I hear she found a way to bring you in line."

"She threatened me with a needle the size of one of Dana's knitting needles."

Sam seemed faintly bemused by that. Penny grinned at him. "I've already asked her to lend it to me."

He scowled at her. "Don't even think about it." He struggled into an upright position and swung his leg off the bed. "Help me up."

She regarded him with astonishment. "Where do you think you're going?"

"Outside. I do not intend to stay cooped up in this room. The sun's shining. I want to be outdoors."

"The doctor doesn't want you climbing stairs."

"Then you shouldn't have stuck me up here, should you? Get my pants."

Penny folded her arms across her chest defiantly. "No."

His gaze narrowed. Finally he shrugged. "Suit yourself."

He stood and the sheet fell away. For the second time in recent weeks Penny was treated to an eyeful. The man was... She searched for a suitable word. Gorgeous didn't seem remotely adequate. Her pulse raced, in spite of her efforts to pretend indifference.

"Sam," she protested.

His eyes glittered with amusement. "Told you to get my pants."

"Hasn't anyone ever introduced you to the concept of underwear?"

"Sure. I've got a whole drawer filled with it."

"You're supposed to wear it."

"In bed? What for?"

Penny groaned. She grabbed his pants off the back of a chair and handed them to him. "If you can get them on by yourself, then we'll talk about going downstairs."

He glowered at her. "I can see why you decided to spend your life with books and germs. You don't know the first thing about getting along with flesh and blood people," he accused as he struggled to stay upright.

"Talk about the pot calling the kettle black," she muttered. It took every ounce of willpower she possessed not to go to his aid as his complexion turned ashen. He finally uttered a sigh of disgust and collapsed back on the bed.

She smiled at him as she gently tugged the sheet back into place. "Maybe tomorrow."

"What am I supposed to do now?"

"Rest."

An oddly wistful expression came over his face. "Sorry. Don't know how."

She realized in a heartbeat that it was probably true. He'd had a tough adolescence and turned into a compulsive overachiever from the day he'd joined the police force.

"When was the last time you took a vacation?"

"I was at the Cape a couple of weeks ago."

"For the weekend," she reminded him.

He shrugged. "That's it."

"You took two consecutive days off and considered it a vacation?"

"Three. I had Friday off, too."

Penny shook her head. "It's going to be a very long recovery, isn't it?"

"For both of us. Is that what you're saying?" He kept his gaze fastened on her when he spoke. "Are you already regretting the fact that you agreed to do this?"

Sam sounded as if it were no more than he had expected, as if he'd known from the outset that she'd run out on him at the first hint of discord. There was a bleak, accepting expression in his eyes that made her want to weep.

Impulsively, she reached out and squeezed his hand. "You're not getting rid of me that easily, Roberts."

She thought she detected a vague hint of relief in his eyes before his eyelids fluttered closed and he drifted off to sleep, still clinging to her hand.

Penny thought perhaps they'd reached an understanding. She'd actually hoped that her reassurances that she wasn't bailing out no matter how difficult he was might actually be a turning point. However, the next day brought absolutely no improvement in Sam's mood.

The arrival of Ryan O'Casey and Jake Washington served as only a minor distraction. Even their announcement that Sam's attackers had been caught and jailed, thanks to an informant in the gang, didn't cheer him up. He seemed to think they should have waited until he could personally capture Tank and his accomplices. Testosterone run amok, Penny thought in disgust.

How could anyone possibly live with a man who dealt with people and danger like that day in and day out, who actually seemed to thrive on it? She was beginning to wonder if she could.

Add in his lousy temper and it was doubtful anyone else would ever be able to pull it off, either. To her surprise, she found herself worrying about him going through life all alone, even though that was what he claimed to want.

Of course, under the circumstances, it could be a very short life. That worried her most of all. Since his attack, she was awakened again and again by nightmares in which he'd been lying in a pool of his own blood, only this time there was no one around to save him. For a long time afterward she'd lain there, bathed in sweat, her heart thudding as she fought off panic.

If she was this terrified now, knowing that he was safe in the bedroom down the hall, what would happen to her when he went back on duty? Her gut-wrenching fear was totally unexpected. In her entire secure existence, she'd never experienced anything like it. She knew it was something she was going to have to confront and confront soon, if she really hoped that one day she and Sam might have a future together.

He regarded her worriedly when she walked into his room the next morning after one of the worst nightmares she'd had. "You okay?" he asked.

"Of course. Why wouldn't I be?"

"I thought I heard you pacing last night."

"Just a bad dream. I couldn't get back to sleep."

"What kind of bad dream?"

She wanted to tell him, wanted him to know how fearful she was, but something in his expression told her he'd already guessed. "It was nothing," she said.

He regarded her bleakly. "If you say so," he said. He rolled onto his side, his back to her, effectively shutting her out.

Penny sighed. Someday soon she would have to be honest with him. For now, though, her only goal was to survive his rotten mood swings, to get him well again.

The next morning before Penny got up, Sam managed to haul himself out of bed and down the stairs. She found him collapsed into a chair on the terrace, his breakfast tray beside him. He stayed where he was, silent and morose, for most of the morning. She could tell when he began getting restless.

He stood and paced back and forth in front of her, until she was ready to scream.

"Sit down and read a book before you tear your stitches open," she advised finally.

He looked as if the concept were alien. She handed him something by Ernest Hemingway that she'd brought out in the distant hope of reading it herself. Maybe he'd buy into all that macho stuff that drove Hemingway's male protagonists.

Fifteen minutes later he'd tossed it aside. "The guy's a jerk," he declared.

"The author or the character?"

"The character," he said at once. Then paused. "Maybe the author. He created the guy, right? Hell, both of them."

To Penny's astonishment, they wound up having an actual conversation about books. It didn't last long, but it was heartening just the same.

When he tired of it, though, he regarded her speculatively. "Want to play poker?"

She caught the unmistakable gleam in his eye. "I don't think so."

He took the refusal in stride. "There are some computer games upstairs. I used to hang out here and play them. Drove Granddad Brandon crazy because he could never beat me. Mrs. Farnsworth told me he used to practice when I wasn't around, cursing a blue streak the whole time.''

''That is not an incentive to get me to take you on,'' Penny told him. ''You're already driving me crazy.''

''I'll go easy on you,'' he promised.

Anything was better than watching him mope around, Penny decided. Besides, it was time to get him back up those stairs and closer to the bed he belonged in.

Fifteen minutes later, she realized to her astonishment that she had a fierce competitive streak. Apparently it had lain dormant all those years when she'd excelled at everything without even trying. Because she also had more patience than Sam, she watched carefully, analyzed the timing of those little characters on the screen and slowly began to get the hang of the game. Once she did that, it was only a little while before she started gaining on him.

''You've played before,'' he accused when she beat him by several hundred points. ''You hustled me.''

''Nope. First time I ever played. It's all a matter of mathematics, timing, maybe some innate coordination.''

She stood. He snagged her hand and pulled her onto his lap. Startled, she stayed where she landed.

''Now let's see if I have this,'' he said.

His gaze was intent in a way that should have made her nervous, but only filled her with an odd little thrill of anticipation.

"One, that's you," he said. "Plus one, that's me, equals two. And if I were to kiss you, say right now, that would be a matter of timing."

Penny seemed to have lost the ability to speak. How had she missed the fact that he was far enough along in his recovery to start thinking about seduction? The man still had a bandage from his collarbone to his belly. Maybe most of his wounds were superficial, but even they weren't fully healed.

His lips curved slightly. "And maybe a little innate coordination, right?"

She swallowed hard. "Right."

"Is there anything I'm missing?"

She shook her head. His gaze softened as his hand curved around the back of her neck.

"This is a really bad idea," he murmured.

Or was that her own conscience screaming? At any rate, it didn't stop the kiss. Nothing short of an air raid siren going off in the next room could have stopped that kiss. It was as inevitable as sunrise.

And, she thought when he left her sitting alone and dazed in front of the computer, it was one damned fine kiss, the kind that could make a less wise woman forget that the man delivering it was flat-out determined to avoid making a commitment.

Chapter Thirteen

Five days of proximity. Five days of Penny's shy, gentle touches and those occasional, dizzying, stolen kisses. Five days of a yearning so powerful that his body felt as if it might ache forever. Sam knew he had misjudged her passion, just as he'd misjudged so much else about her... and about himself.

Determined not to let these discoveries affect him, he actually tried to tell himself that his desire was purely physical, the result of remaining celibate too damn long. He hadn't looked at another woman since Penny had arrived on the scene in Boston. He tried to tell himself that that was sheer coincidence. He tried to tell himself that under those circumstances any woman would have aroused the same desperate hunger.

He wondered when he'd turned into such a liar.

It was Penny who exasperated and enchanted him. It was Penny who filled his dreams. It was Penny whose most casual caress made his pulse race. It was Penny who was going to drive him out of his head with longing if he didn't do something about it.

The quickest, surest way to solve the immediate problem would be to get her into his bed. Given the fact that she was still worriedly hovering over it half a dozen times a day, even though the doctor had said he was virtually back to normal, it shouldn't be that difficult to tumble her into it.

Sam considered the matter with detached, calculating, masculine logic. One quick roll in the hay and he'd be over her. The intrigue would be over. That was the way it usually worked for him. There was no connection whatsoever between his brain and his libido.

As for a heart, everyone knew he didn't have one. He saw no reason for this time to be any different. It was just the noble, hands-off policy he'd adopted that was making her so blasted tempting. A person always wanted most what he couldn't have, what he wouldn't allow himself to have.

He tried to convince himself that seducing her wouldn't be such a lousy thing to do. After all, this hunger wasn't entirely one-sided. There was an undeniable mutual attraction between them. There had been from the start.

Sam had seen the flare of unmistakable excitement in Penny's eyes each time they'd kissed. He'd felt the way she responded in his arms. More important, they were both smart enough to recognize that they were too different to ever have a lasting relationship. They'd both be better off if they just had sex and got it over with.

Sam was still in the midst of the greatest internal moral debate of his entire life, when Penny sashayed into his bedroom looking like a ray of sunshine and humming some cheerful little tune. She was wildly off key and clearly couldn't have cared less.

She wore seductive white shorts and a clingy, yellow T-shirt. She'd scooped her hair into a ponytail with some sort of bright yellow scarf thing. He gazed down and saw that she was barefoot and sometime since he'd last seen her she had painted her toenails an enticing, feminine shade of pink. He suddenly felt an overwhelming urge to kiss each and every one of them. Dear heaven, he was losing his mind, he thought with dismay.

Hands on hips, she stood over him. "Are you okay?" she inquired worriedly. "You look funny."

He shifted in the bed, turning onto his side. "Funny how?" he asked cautiously, hoping she hadn't seen the erection that she'd aroused just by walking into the room.

"All flushed and feverish. I'd better take your temperature."

She whipped a thermometer out of her pocket and removed the cap. He shoved it away. He was overheated all right, but he doubted it would register on the instrument. "Forget it. I'm fine."

"But you could have an infection. I'll call the doctor to stop by and check your bandages."

"Take it from me, sweetheart. It's not an infection."

Something in his tone must have alerted her. She might not be an experienced lover, but she'd certainly taken enough science courses to understand basic anatomy and human chemistry. Her gaze shot to the telltale bulge beneath the sheet. The expression of fascination on her face, combined with the flood of color into her cheeks, were almost his undoing. His entire body throbbed with sexual awareness.

Eventually her gaze returned to meet his. To his amazement and vague alarm, he detected a faint hint of amusement. It was the last reaction he'd anticipated.

"Are you absolutely sure there is nothing I can help you with?" she inquired in a voice that had suddenly dropped to a sultry, sensual purr.

"Penny," he warned, guessing that his plan was about to go dangerously astray.

"Yes, Sam," she replied, her blue eyes wide with feigned innocence.

"Don't pull that act with me. You have picked a very bad time to turn into a flirt."

"Oh, really? I thought my timing was downright excellent." She glanced back at the evidence to prove

it. Sam groaned and waged one last battle with himself. He lost.

He reached out and snagged her hand. "Closer,"
he urged.

"You sound like the big, bad wolf talking to Little
Red Riding Hood."

"There are certain similarities in our situations,"
he agreed. His hand tightened around hers. "Games
are over, Penny. Now's the time to back out if you
don't want to play."

Her lower lip trembled slightly, but her chin jutted
up and she shook her head. Sam looked into her eyes
and thought he saw a longing there that reflected his
own. Maybe it was only his own wishful thinking, the
justification he needed for going on with his plan. He
didn't waste time trying to analyze it.

"Jeez," he muttered. "When you look at me like
that, I don't think I could send you away if our lives
depended on it."

"Then don't," she said, her gaze never wavering.

"Where's Mrs. Farnsworth?"

"I sent her off on a list of errands that ought to
keep her occupied past nightfall."

"Good," he said softly.

Her foresight told him she'd been anticipating
something like this. Knowing that, the last of his already tattered willpower melted. With one tug, he
pulled her onto the bed beside him. She sat there, stiff
and still, waiting, expectant. He lifted his hand and
removed the band holding her hair. When it tumbled

loose, he ran his fingers through it. It felt like silk, just as he'd anticipated.

"I knew it," he murmured, filled with the same awe he'd experienced the first time Brandon Halloran had taken him on a tour of Halloran Industries' finest fabrics.

A smile flitted across her lips. "Knew what?"

"How your hair would feel. I remember when I first touched strands of silk at Halloran Industries. I couldn't believe that anything could be that fine, that delicate. It felt just like this."

His old fascination with textures, a fascination instilled by Brandon's love of quality materials, came over him. He caressed her cheek. "And your skin, it's like the finest satin, but warmer."

He trailed a caress along her neck, lingering where he felt the rapid flutter of her pulse. "Scared?" he asked quietly. He didn't see any signs of it, but he needed to ask.

She shook her head in a denial that wasn't quite matched by the racing of her heartbeat.

"Of you? Never," she swore, anyway.

"Maybe you should be. I love 'em and leave 'em," he warned matter-of-factly. "Everybody knows that. Nobody expects anything more."

She flinched slightly at that, but he could detect the instant when her resolve returned. "I'm living very much in the present. Whatever the future holds, I'll deal with it."

At that precise moment, listening to her brave declaration, feeling her skin heat beneath his touch, Sam thought he could very well fall in love with her... if he was the kind of man who believed in love. As it was, though, he knew for a fact that there was no such thing as some romantic destiny.

Penny watched the carefully banked emotion in Sam's eyes and knew that he was fighting feeling anything more than his sexual attraction for her. The struggle gave her hope.

The man actually thought this seduction had been his idea. In reality, she'd done everything short of leaving a stack of *Playboys* beside his bed to stir him up. She might be new to the game, she might not understand all the rules, but Sam had a very transparent face. She knew exactly when she was getting to him and each time she did, she contrived to do more of the same. Little had been left to chance, from the outfit she'd chosen this morning to the dismissal of the housekeeper for the day. She'd known his recovery was almost complete for days now. Both of them had been drawing out this torment of living under the same roof.

What she was doing was not without risk. He could make love to her, decide that it satisfied what had been no more than a momentary whim and never see her again. Or it could wake him up to the fact that they were meant to be together, that what they felt was deep and true and lasting.

She wished to heaven she had more experience in making sex absolutely unforgettable. As it was, she had a rudimentary understanding of the basics and no practical experience whatsoever beyond a few steamy kisses and an occasional groping touch that had done nothing to inflame her. She knew things with Sam were going to be different for her because his most innocent touch set her afire. But would they be different enough for a man who used and discarded women like tissues and actually prided himself on that fact?

Right now his hand had strayed to her breast, where the most astonishing sensations were ricocheting from there to her toes and back again. "Sam?"

His gaze was pinned on hers. "Yes, sweetheart."

"Isn't it possible that I have on too many clothes?"

He grinned at her. "That depends on how fast you intend to move things along."

"I think I might be in a hurry."

"Then by all means take off anything you like."

Thrilled by the flare of excitement that shone in his eyes, she lifted her T-shirt over her head and tossed it onto the floor. But when she reached for the clasp of her bra, he nudged her hands aside.

"Allow me."

The brush of his fingertips along her bare midriff was an exquisite form of torture. When his hands settled on her back, he was close enough that she could feel the whisper of his breath across her cheek. It seemed to her that he lingered over the task far longer than it required, turning it into a sweet torment.

As soon as he'd unhooked the bra, he looped his hands beneath it, brought it off her shoulders and allowed it to fall away, exposing her breasts. First his thumb, then his mouth traced the outline where the lacy material had been. Penny's pulse scrambled at the touch of his tongue against her nipple. She was sure that that intimate contact alone was going to send her spinning off into an aching ecstasy.

But it was just the beginning. Despite her frantic desire for urgency, Penny watched his face to make sure none of this was too taxing. He seemed so... intent. He took his own sweet time with every touch. It seemed as if he'd made the sensitizing of her breasts his single most important task of the day. With slow deliberation, he tasted and savored and teased until Penny was ready to scream with need. All the time he watched her face, his own expression was a blend of fascination and satisfaction that filled her with feminine pride.

"You're something else," he whispered, his voice husky and dark as midnight.

Penny felt as if he'd given her the moon. Now, though, she had this consuming need to claim the stars, as well. "I want you," she told him. "Please, Sam."

He stripped away her shorts and panties far more efficiently than he had her bra. When she was completely bare, though, he resumed the slow, tortuous process of making her tremble with desire. His hands molded, caressed and teased, dipping into her moist warmth with an intense probing that had her hips lifting off the bed to meet each intimate touch.

She hadn't expected the spiraling tension, the vague but constant striving toward some elusive goal. Each touch was an experience like nothing she'd ever felt before. And each one made her crave more. There was no time to savor the joy of each new sensation. Always there was the unconscious struggle to reach the challenging peak that promised to be more spectacular than fireworks and roller coaster rides all blended into one incredible moment.

"Sam?" It came out as a soft plea.

"I know, sweetheart. You're ready, aren't you?"

"I think I've been waiting for this all my life," she murmured solemnly.

He braced himself above her then and she could feel the tip of his manhood as he slowly began to ease inside. Again his gaze was locked with hers, his face a study in concentration.

"You okay?" he asked.

She offered him a tremulous smile. "Never better. But if you don't get on with this, I think I may fly apart."

A grin tugged at his lips. "We can't have that happening, can we? At least not without me along for the ride."

His next thrust was fast and hard. Penny felt the momentary resistance, the quick, burning pain, and then...the most awesome sense of completion she had ever felt in her life. A magical union that was meant to be. Tentatively she lifted her hips and began a rhythm as old as time.

"You're remarkable," Sam whispered.

Those two words filled her heart just as he had filled her body. She stroked his shoulders, hesitating when her fingers met the bandages on his chest. Struck anew by worry, she looked into his eyes.

"I'm fine," he reassured. "More than fine."

To prove it, he increased the rhythm to a pace just shy of unbearable. That nagging tension spiralled tighter and tighter, before finally ripping free in a glorious burst of excitement.

When the release of her first climax spread over Penny in wave after wave of thrilling sensation, she thought she knew without a doubt the timeless meaning of love. Two people, joined as one—heart, body and soul. Not even Sam, stubborn, tender, arrogant Sam, could walk away from something this powerful.

He'd ruined everything, Sam decided later that night as he paced his room. Penny was back in her own room. Mrs. Farnsworth had returned to her duties. Everything was going on exactly as if nothing had happened. But it had, and now he didn't know what the hell to do about it.

He hadn't meant to kiss her. He hadn't even meant to see her again. He sure as hell hadn't meant to have sex with her. And he certainly hadn't expected it to be the most thrilling, passionate sex of his entire life.

Okay, this was no time to be dishonest. He *had* meant to seduce her. He'd decided on it coldly and pragmatically as a solution to his own frustration. He just hadn't meant to get caught up in its trap. He hadn't meant for it to mean anything to him at all.

But she'd looked so inviting, so soft and feminine and downright sexy with that triumphant smirk of satisfaction on her face. She had been so willing, so responsive in his arms. He had taken pride in the mechanics of satisfying her, but more importantly he had felt a sense of wonder for the first time since he'd lost his own virginity a dozen years ago.

And somewhere between the first kiss and the final tumultuous explosion of their shared climax, Sam had realized that Penny was not going to be so easy to get out of his system. She'd sneaked into his heart and that, the experts were likely to say, was what had made the difference between this time and all the others. How it had happened was beyond him. They were nothing alike.

Maybe he just had a thing for winners, women who took what they wanted in life and exulted in it. Penny was such a woman. He had seen it in her face. He had felt joyous, but she had looked absolutely triumphant at the moment he had come apart in her arms. He supposed it was the natural order of things. People wanted what they didn't have. Losers wanted to win. Loners wanted love, whether they cared to admit it or not.

He, however, had no intention of admitting to such a need. Not even now. It had been a momentary aberration, nothing more. He was a loner. In time, these feelings he had for Penny would fade.

Of course, if Brandon Halloran ever found out about what had gone on in this bedroom, he probably wouldn't even care how Sam viewed his future.

Brandon would sail into Boston with a ring tucked in his pocket and a reservation at the chapel where Halloran weddings were always triumphantly celebrated.

The only way to avoid not only that, but any further temptation, though, was to sneak out of this house, which had known its share of love. It was essential that he get back to his own bachelor quarters, where no woman would dare to intrude. He had to reclaim the solitary existence that had always suited him just fine.

The plan of action decided, Sam found it was a struggle just to get into his clothes. It was more of a strain to get down the stairs. The worst struggle was pretending that his going wouldn't matter to either one of them.

He overcame each and every struggle, each and every guilty second thought. He called a taxi and was gone by dawn, satisfied that what he'd done was for the best.

And, not one hour later, just when he was soundly asleep, confident that his leaving would demonstrate to Penny once and for all what a rotten bet he was, the pounding on his door proved the error of his assumptions. He had no doubt that the person on the other side of his threshhold was the very woman he'd intended to avoid for the rest of his days.

"I know you're in there, Sam Roberts," she shouted. "Open the damn door."

She sounded royally ticked off. He had to admire the gumption it had taken for her to storm across town and confront him. Reluctantly he opened the door.

She stood there, eyes blazing with fury, her hair a tangled mess, her clothes obviously assembled hastily. Almost nothing matched. She seemed oblivious to the picture she presented. Something deep inside Sam twisted at the sight of her. She was going to be difficult to get out of his system, all right. Even looking as if she'd dressed from a ragbag, she turned his heart to mush.

"You fool!" she said, waving a finger in his face as she marched toward him.

"How'd you know where I was?" he asked, stalling for time.

"Where else would you go? No one else in the family would put up with you and you're too weak to crawl onto a plane and head for parts unknown. Mrs. Farnsworth gave me the address."

Sam acknowledged the truth of that with a sigh. Then the confrontation took an amazing twist when she backed him into a corner and berated him not for endangering his life—though she did that, too—but for running scared.

"You're a low-down coward," she accused, jabbing her finger toward his belly, but stopping just short of contact.

"A coward?" he repeateded incredulously. "Just exactly what am I supposed to be scared of?"

"Me," she announced with no hesitation whatsoever.

Sam's spirits sank. So, he thought with a weary sigh of resignation, she had him pegged, after all. Even before he'd realized it himself, she had guessed that he was falling in love with the little brat. Correct that. With the grown-up, incredibly sexy, little brat.

What she apparently hadn't grasped quite yet was the fact that he had absolutely no intention whatsoever of doing anything about it.

Chapter Fourteen

Penny stood in the middle of Sam's cluttered living room, oblivious to her surroundings, as he explained to her precisely why there could never be anything between them. He eliminated her theory—his own ridiculous fear of commitment—and blamed it on personality differences, background differences and a host of other reasons that made about as much sense as a baby's first babbling words. To hear him tell it, they barely spoke the same language. About midway through the recitation, Penny lost patience.

"And where were these differences a few hours ago when we were together in bed?" she inquired bluntly.

"The only difference that mattered there was the gender difference," he retorted.

He deliberately avoided her gaze when he said it, probably because he knew she'd laugh in his face. He wasn't finished, though. He still had more to say on the subject, as if he thought the sheer volume of words would convince her of something that was utter hogwash.

"But we can't spend our whole lives in bed. There has to be more than that between us."

"And you don't think there is?"

"I'm a cop, Penny. You live in some safe, academic ivory tower. You've been terrified ever since those punks attacked me. My world just isn't your world."

She regarded him incredulously. "What kind of garbage is that? Have you heard me utter one single word about being afraid? Have you heard me beg you to quit the force?"

His jaw set, he met her gaze evenly. "Maybe not, but it's the truth."

"You're a mind reader now?"

"I know what I saw in your eyes in the hospital. I know what all the nightmares were about at Brandon's. Why can't you admit it?"

She drew in a breath and tried to respond calmly and rationally to what seemed to her a very irrational theory. "Okay, yes, I was scared every time I thought about what might have happened that night. You could have died. Being frightened by that seems like a pretty sensible reaction to me."

"I won't have you living in fear on my account," he insisted stubbornly. "Someday you'll thank me."

A weary sigh of resignation shuddered through her. "And someday you'll regret what you've thrown away," she said quietly.

Penny could see it was useless trying to make Sam see sense. She'd taken a risk by making love with him and she'd lost. She would not stand here and beg the man to commit to a future he obviously couldn't envision. If he intended to be arrogant and willful and downright stupid, that was his problem. She would not let it be hers.

She thought back over all the years she had wasted worrying that Sam's rejection meant there was something wrong with her. Now she knew that it had been him all along. He was the one who couldn't cope with real intimacy, who didn't even want to try because the fear of being abandoned ate at him every day of his life. Talk about someone living in terror.

She took one last look at him, drinking in the sight of his sexy, shadowed complexion, the body that had given her her first taste of physical pleasure, the eyes that hinted of a vulnerability that he would deny with his last breath.

She also saw the pallor, the unsteadiness of his hand as he raked his fingers through his hair, and was afraid for him. He was rushing his recuperation, and without her around to intercede, who knew what risks he'd take.

"I'll send the nurse over to check on you tomorrow," she said finally. "You look like hell."

"Don't bother. I'm going back to work."

"You can't work in this condition," she protested, then bit off the rest of the lecture as his jaw clenched. She shrugged. "Do what you want. It's your life."

She stared at him until he was finally forced to meet her gaze. "I hope it's a good one," she said quietly. "I wish only the best for you. Like it or not, Sam Roberts, I love you. Nothing you do or say is going to change that."

Then, because she knew it wasn't this moment but the future that scared him, she added emphatically, "I will always love you."

There was a flicker of reaction in his eyes, but he remained stoically silent, killing any last chance they might have had. Penny turned her back on him then and walked out the door. It was the hardest thing she'd ever done in her life.

She made it out the door before her throat clogged with emotion and her eyes swam with tears. At the end of the hall, she leaned against the wall and tried to gather her composure. Hot tears of frustration spilled down her cheeks. She wiped at them angrily and swore they would be the last she shed for a man who didn't want her, a man who had never cared... not enough, anyway.

Finally she drew in a shaky breath, squared her shoulders and marched down the stairs. She had a life to get back to and she was determined it was going to be a fantastic one. What was it Dorothy Parker had written? Something about living well being the best revenge. She intended to have her revenge on Sam Roberts, even if it killed her.

Sam listened to Penny's fading footsteps with a dull ache in his chest. She was going. She was walking out of his life without a backward glance. He should have felt victorious, or at the very least, relieved. Instead the encounter had left him drained, his head throbbing. He felt this terrible sense of loss that he wanted very much to blame on her.

What had he expected? he asked himself irritably. He was the one who'd sent her away. Had he expected her to fight like a hellion? Had he expected her to counter all of his absurd excuses for ending things between them?

Okay, so maybe some tiny little part of him had wanted just that. Oh, sure, he had turned aside every argument she had tried to make, but they were pitiful. Besides, he knew in his gut that whatever it was they were feeling wasn't powerful enough to last. He'd just tested it and proved that, hadn't he? They were both better off knowing the truth.

But he didn't feel better off somehow. He felt like hell, as if he'd cheated both of them of something important.

As he'd threatened, he went back to work the next day. His boss took one look at him and sent him back home.

"Next time you come back, I want a signed release from your doctor," he told Sam. "I'm not going to have you or one of your fellow officers wind up shot because your reflexes are worth spit."

"I need to get back on the job," Sam argued with a sense of desperation.

"Then go home and recuperate so you can do it."

"I'll work a desk."

"And drive us all nuts complaining about it. I don't think so. Go home and get well so you can get back to doing what you do best. With Tank in jail, his gang is floundering. We can get in there and clean up the last dregs as soon as you're back on the streets."

Sam knew his boss was right. He was so exhausted from the trip to the station that he could barely make it up the stairs when he got home. He unplugged the phone and collapsed onto his bed. Drained both physically and mentally, he slept practically around the clock.

It was midmorning the next day when he heard someone fiddling with his lock. Sam was reaching for his gun when he recognized Mrs. Farnsworth's voice, then Randy's. The pairing should have astonished him, but nothing much surprised him anymore.

"Thank you, young man," the housekeeper said. "You're quite adept with that instrument. What was it you called it? A picklock?"

"Yeah, well, it might be better if we don't tell Sam how we got in," Randy replied nervously.

Sam chuckled despite himself. He leaned back against the pillows and waited for whatever the two had in store for him.

"You can run along now," Mrs. Farnsworth said. "I'm certain you have things to do."

"Are you sure you don't want me to check the place out? He could be real sick or something."

"I'm certain I can handle whatever the situation is," she said firmly.

Sam doubted there was anything on earth that Mrs. Farnsworth couldn't handle after decades of battling wits with Brandon Halloran, but to his amazement she suddenly relented. He suspected Randy had put on his most woebegone expression. The door to his room inched open.

"Sam?" Randy whispered. "Hey, Sam!"

Sam remained steadfastly silent.

"I think he's passed out or something," Randy announced.

There was that *or something* again, Sam thought with a grin. He hoped the kid wasn't going to be disappointed to find him very much alive.

Suddenly the door was thrown wide and Mrs. Farnsworth strode across the room. She loomed over him, her expression set in a disapproving frown. "Sam Roberts, stop playing possum. You're scaring that poor boy to death."

He winked at her. "How'd you know I wasn't dead?"

"Because you're entirely too ornery to die this young."

Randy crept into the room and regarded him with an injured expression. "Why'd you go and do that?"

"Do what?" Sam asked innocently. "I was sleeping peacefully in my own apartment when two people broke in. You're lucky I didn't shoot you."

"You didn't answer the phone or the door," Randy countered. "How come?"

"Maybe I didn't want to talk to anybody."

"That's typical of your selfishness, young man," Mrs. Farnsworth chided. "Folks have been worried sick about you and you've been holed up in here sulking."

"Who says I'm sulking? I just told you I was sleeping. Anyway, why were you checking on me in the first place?"

"Beats me," she said. "Some people were foolish enough to care what happened to you."

"Which people?" he asked because he couldn't help himself.

She gave him an inscrutable look. "Me for one. Isn't that enough?"

"You're a treasure, Mrs. F."

A smile teased her stern lips, but she fought it admirably. "You haven't called me that in a long time." She scowled at him. "Won't make a bit of difference, though. I'm still tired of your foolishness. I should have sent Ruth Dawkins over here with that needle of hers."

Sam took the threat seriously. He mustered an apology. "I'm sorry if I worried you," he said. "And anyone else who might have been concerned."

"Yes, well, it seems to me like you might have more than one thing to apologize to her for."

Sam stared at her, thoroughly startled. "What do you know?" he asked worriedly.

"Enough," she said succinctly. She opened a Thermos of soup and poured some into a bowl. "Eat this."

Randy was watching the housekeeper with a speculative look in his eyes. She glanced at him.

"If you want some, go into the kitchen and get a bowl," she said. After he'd gone, she said, "That boy needs a family. He has some skills that bear watching."

"An understatement if ever I heard one," Sam agreed.

"Perhaps I'll have a talk with Mr. Halloran. I'm sure he wouldn't mind if the boy stayed at the house for a while. It's empty most of the time, anyway."

Sam reached for her hand and squeezed. "You're a wonder, Mrs. F."

"Just doing my Christian duty."

He shook his head. "It's more than that. I just want you to know I appreciate it. Randy's worth saving. I can remember when I was a lot like him. Granddad Brandon came to my rescue."

She leveled a stern look at him. "The boy thinks the world of you. Did you know he was just hanging around outside in case you needed him? Found him sitting out there on the front steps."

"How'd he know I was back here?"

"Same way I knew to bring the soup. Penny." She regarded him intently. "She's good for you. Don't throw away a chance at happiness. You've always taken every risk there was to be taken. Don't stop now."

Sam sighed. "I love you for caring, Mrs. F., but you don't know what you're talking about."

"I didn't get to be this age without learning a thing or two," she retorted. "You'd be wise to listen to your elders once in a while. We didn't do too badly by you in the past, did we?"

"No," he conceded.

"Well, then?"

"I'll think about what you've said. I promise."

But the minute she was gone, he stubbornly put the promise out of his head.

A week later Dana turned up on his doorstep, her two littlest ones in tow. Within fifteen minutes, the kids were out of control and whatever Dana had stopped by to say had been overshadowed by the chaos. His head throbbing again, Sam cheerfully considered murdering them and his meddlesome sister.

Dana scooped up the screaming baby and held her out to him. "Hold your niece while I chase after her brother."

Sam had the baby cradled in his arms before he could protest. "You sound like I feel," he told Jennifer Margaret Halloran. "I wouldn't mind letting off a little steam myself. What has you so upset?"

Serious blue eyes swimming with tears stared back at him. The baby hiccuped, then quieted. The kid really was beautiful, he decided with total objectivity, even if she was still bald. And she already had the good sense to know when she was in the care of someone big and strong, who'd protect her with his life. That instinctively trusting response was worrisome. He'd done his damnedest to prove to everyone that he wasn't reliable. He supposed Jennifer Margaret would learn that lesson soon enough.

"I see you've worked your magic on her, just the way you do on all the girls," Dana commented when she reappeared.

She looked slightly more frazzled than she had when she'd left. She had Jason Junior in tow. The two-year-old seemed pleased with the amount of toothpaste he'd been able to smear all over himself in his few minutes of freedom from parental interference.

"Shave," he announced happily, patting his round little cheeks.

"Why didn't somebody tell me that boys are a lot more difficult to control than girls?" Dana muttered while trying to clean up her son.

"Hey, you were the one who raised me. That should have been warning enough."

"Very funny." She regarded him pensively. "So, little brother, let's get serious. Exactly what's standing between you and Penny? It's obvious to everyone that you're in love with her. It's also clear that for some absurd reason you've decided to shut her out of your life."

"Did she tell you that?"

"No. She's just as tight-lipped about all this as you are, but she's got circles under her eyes and she's losing weight she can't spare. Stop torturing her and yourself and admit how you really feel."

"If you came by to tout the thrills of marriage, you should have left the munchkins at home," he retorted dryly.

Dana waved her hand dismissively. "Don't give me that. You adore them, even when they're screaming and soggy. It's not my kids who have you scared senseless. It's the prospect of commitment, isn't it?"

Sam really didn't want to get into this. Unfortunately, knowing his sister, he wasn't going to have a choice. "Let's face it, Dana, we didn't have much of an example," he said finally. "We don't even know if our father is alive or not."

She didn't deny it. "I've overcome that," she reminded him.

"Yeah, well, I haven't. Besides, the guy you got was one in a million. He's let you be yourself."

"Are you suggesting that Penny won't let you be yourself?"

"She hates the fact that I'm a cop."

"Has she asked you to give it up?"

"No," he admitted.

"Couldn't it be that she's just afraid of losing you? Isn't that natural? I'm terrified every time I think about you getting involved in some dangerous undercover assignment. I spent hours in that hospital waiting room ranting and raving about getting you off the force if you survived this last time. Ask Jason about the threats I made. But the bottom line is, you can't protect us from fear."

"But I don't have to see the fear in your eyes," he said bleakly. "Penny tries so damned hard not to let me see how scared she is, but it's always there. She was the most trusting, innocent human being in the world until she met me. She loved people, believed in their innate goodness. Being with a cop has made her see the rotten side of things, things she shouldn't have to know about. She'd never even seen a guy like Tank before she came here, much less been victimized by one."

"Don't you think you're being a little hard on yourself? Not everyone in the world is good and kind, and Penny was awfully naive if she believed that they were. Maybe it was time she took off her blinders, if she ever had them on in the first place. Los Angeles isn't exactly a crime-free mecca of serenity."

He refused to be swayed. "A man's supposed to protect the woman he loves from the bad things, not bring her smack into the midst of them."

"Is that how she feels?"

"She must. Just look what happened with Tank."

"He hurt you, not her."

"If she feels the way you seem to think she does, I'm not sure she'd see the distinction. Besides, for a while there he was after her."

"And you stopped him from getting anywhere near her," she countered reasonably.

"It was my fault he was after her in the first place."

She regarded him with exasperation. "Oh, for heaven's sake, will you give it a rest. That's over, done with, kaput. The sleaze is in jail. It has nothing to do with the future.''

"There are a lot of kids like Tank in the world."

"And a lot more like Randy. And like my munch-kins," she reminded him. "I still say you should be asking Penny how she feels about it."

"I know how she feels."

She shot him a look filled with disbelief. "Oh, re-ally? Have you actually asked? Never mind. I know the answer. You're just going to make that decision for her, because you think you, the almighty male, must know what's best for her." She shook her head, clearly disgusted. "Get real, Sammy. If she's smart enough for you to fall in love with her, then she's smart enough to make her own decisions."

"You may be right," he admitted, carefully plac-ing the baby back into her carrier. "But I won't take that kind of chance."

He leaned down and brushed a kiss across Dana's furrowed brow. "Stop worrying, sis. You and the munchkins are enough family for me."

"If you believe that, Sam Roberts, then you're a bigger fool than I ever imagined."

He winked at her. "Could be."

"Sammy!"

"Later, sis."

"You can't walk out on company."

"Sure I can. I've got things to do. Besides, you're family. You'll understand."

He could hear Jennifer Margaret's wailing and Dana's curses all the way down the hall. Despite the fact that he was the target of their protests, he found himself chuckling. He seemed to be surrounded by women of all ages who thought they knew what was best for him and had no hesitation whatsoever about expressing it.

Chapter Fifteen

Some pull that Sam couldn't have defined if his life had depended on it drew him to Penny's lab a few nights later. He had a long list of excuses. He ticked them off.

It was a hot, muggy evening.

His apartment was like an oven.

He needed to get out, try to find a breeze.

He had cabin fever.

He needed a long walk to get his strength back.

He was getting restless after being cooped up for days on end.

Dana's worried phone calls were getting to him and the only way to escape them was to get away from the damn phone.

Oh, he had lots of reasons for getting out of the apartment, all right. Not one of them mentioned anything about going by the lab.

Destination or not, that's where he wound up. Once there, he tried to convince himself that all he wanted was a quick glimpse of Penny, just to make sure she was okay. It didn't seem to matter that Tank was in jail. Sam hadn't been able to shake the feeling that something was wrong and that it was up to him to discover what that might be. The past couple of weeks had to have been traumatic for her and most of the blame for that was his. He had a responsibility to make sure she'd gotten over it, right?

Yeah, right. But no matter how he tried to explain it away in rational terms, this sudden compulsion to come by the lab tonight worried him. Had he gotten so used to looking out for her, to caring about what happened to her, that he couldn't give it up, after all, even though there was nothing personal between them?

Nothing personal, he mocked. Vivid, erotic images came back to haunt him with stunning clarity. He tried to block the memories with every last shred of willpower he possessed. He wondered if Penny was having the same difficulty. And if she was, if he was her single biggest problem, how would he handle that?

He lingered in the shadows, watching as the lights went out in the lab, waiting for her to exit the building. Suddenly, to his deep regret, Randy materialized beside him.

"How come you're here?" the teenager de-manded. "I thought you and Ms. Hayden had a fight."

There was no mistaking the accusing note in his voice. "It wasn't a fight," Sam replied defensively. "Not exactly. Look, it's between Penny and me, okay?"

"You made her cry."

The knife in Sam's heart twisted. The last thing he'd been looking for tonight was someone else to lay the blame for this mess squarely on his doorstep. "How do you know that?"

"I saw her."

"But what makes you think it had anything to do with me?"

Randy regarded him with supreme disgust. "I asked, man. That's how you find out stuff."

"And she actually told you that she was crying over me?"

The teenager shook his head. "What she said was that some men were destined to go through life all alone unless they learned to deal with their feelings. She told me never to be afraid to say what was in my heart. You know, mushy stuff like that."

"And from that you figured that she was crying over me?" Sam said with amazement.

"Well, who else could she mean? You're the only man she worries about." He looked uneasy. "At least, you were."

Sam pinned him with a look. "What does that mean?"

"There's this guy, a doctor, I think. She's been with him almost every night after work."

"The same one you mentioned before," Sam said sarcastically, reminding Randy of the made-up suitor he had used to try to get a rise out of Sam. The last time it had worked. Not again.

"Nah, this one's real." Randy gestured toward the lab. "See."

Sure enough, Penny was emerging from the building, chatting with some guy wearing a white lab coat, a stethoscope tucked in his pocket. He was tall and distinguished-looking, the kind of substantial, well-connected man she deserved, Sam decided, forcing himself to be objective.

He couldn't seem to take his eyes off of her. She was wearing a summer dress he hadn't seen before, one that bared her delectable shoulders. Sam's gut tied itself in knots. He wanted to shout at her to put on the jacket she was carrying over one arm. He wanted to kiss the exposed skin until she trembled. Damn!

Something the man said made her laugh. Sam could hear the carefree sound floating on the breeze. His heart ached that the laughter hadn't been meant for his ears.

When the doctor casually draped his arm across her shoulders, a primitive, possessive rage roared through Sam. Every instinct told him to walk over there and claim her, but he remained right where he was, as if rooted there for eternity.

"What are you going to do about it?" Randy asked, watching him hopefully.

"Nothing," Sam said bleakly. He'd known this day would come eventually, had expected it, in fact. What he hadn't anticipated was how soon it would be and how much it would hurt.

"*Nothing?* Come on, man. You don't want to lose her."

"She's not mine to lose."

Randy regarded him with disgust. "Jeez, I guess that leaves it up to me."

Before Sam could stop him, Randy took off at a run, joining the couple as they started down the block. Penny greeted him with a smile, linking her arm through his, while Sam's stomach churned with envy.

But as badly as he wanted to, he couldn't make himself go after them. She was better off without him. They both knew that. At least, he did, and she would figure it out soon enough.

Since Sam couldn't follow them, he wandered back the way he'd come and spent the rest of the evening in his apartment downing Scotch in place of the painkillers he'd stopped days earlier. It left him not only disgruntled and depressed, but almost guaranteed a miserable hangover. He figured that was pretty much what he deserved for being such a damn fool. How had he allowed himself, even for a moment, to believe that anything as special as what he and Penny had shared the past few weeks could possibly last? He was the son of Paul Roberts, a man who hadn't known the first thing about commitment, a man who'd deserted his wife and children. The same sorry genes were at work in him.

"Have you had dinner yet?" Penny asked Randy when they were back in her neighborhood.

She wasn't sure she could bear another evening alone. All she did was worry about Sam and make herself sick wondering what she could have done to make things turn out differently. She'd been thrilled when Randy had come along just as she was on her way home.

"Not really," Randy said.

"Let's go to Rosie's, then. My treat." She gazed into his troubled brown eyes. "Do you have time?"

"Sure. It's just that…isn't that where you and Sam used to go?"

Struck by his amazingly mature sensitivity, she squeezed his hand. "Hey, it's okay. I'm not going to get all teary-eyed on you again."

"I don't care if you cry," he said, turning red. "I mean, I don't mind if you do it around me. I just don't like for you to be sad."

"I have no intention of letting Sam Roberts make me sad ever again," she vowed.

Randy looked skeptical. "If you say so." He glanced up at her, his expression sly. "I saw him tonight."

"Is he okay?" she asked at once, without thinking of how Randy would view the automatic response.

Randy grinned. "You guys are pathetic. You can't go five minutes without asking about him. He can't go five minutes without worrying about you. But you won't see each other. I don't get it."

Frankly, Penny wasn't so sure she got it, either. "It's just the way it is," she said wearily.

"But it doesn't have to be that way. You should have seen the way he looked when he saw you with the doc tonight."

"Sam saw us? He was at the lab?"

"Waiting around outside," Randy confirmed. "It made him crazy when he saw you with another guy. I didn't tell him that you usually just walk to the bus stop together. He thought it was like a date or something."

Penny sighed. It might have made Sam crazy, but he hadn't done anything about it. He was still refusing to acknowledge his feelings for her, and as long as he was so blasted determined to remain aloof, there was nothing she could do.

"Well?" Randy prodded. "Don't you think that means something? He looked really angry. That must mean he cares, right?"

"Believe me, if I understood the way Sam's mind worked, we wouldn't be in this mess. Come on. I'm starved," she said, pointedly changing the subject.

Randy regarded her with obvious disappointment, but that was nothing compared to the expression on Rosie's face when she learned that Sam would not be joining them.

"What is the matter with him? Did that crazy boy with the knife do something to his brain? No. The cut was to his stomach, but it has affected his mind." She patted Penny's hand. "Do not worry. I will fix this."

Oh, Lord, Penny thought. *First Randy, now Rosie. Add in Brandon, Dana and whoever else felt inclined to meddle and Sam was likely to head for Wyoming and take up cattle ranching.*

"Please. Let it be," she pleaded. "He has to work this out for himself."

"He is a man," Rosie declared with disdain. "They do not work things out. They sulk like little boys. They need to be pushed into doing what is right."

The idea of anyone pushing Sam into doing anything he didn't want to do made Penny smile.

"See," Rosie declared triumphantly. "You agree."

"No. Yes. Oh, for heaven's sake, Rosie, you know Sam better than I do. Has he ever taken advice from anyone?"

Rosie frowned. "No," she conceded.

"He rebels, right?"

"Yes."

"Then it's best to leave him alone."

Rosie regarded her worriedly. "You will wait for him to make up his mind?"

Penny shrugged. "I don't really have any choice. I've fallen in love with the hardheaded jerk."

"All right!" Randy said, beaming at her and giving a high-five to Rosie.

Penny glared at them. She was delighted to see that they thought it mattered one whit what she felt. Sam was the troublesome one, not her.

The phone call came several days later at an incredibly impolite hour, after midnight. However, it was only nine-thirty in California and Penny guessed even before she heard the voice on the other end of the line that it would be her grandfather. Obviously he'd made the call late at night her time in the vain hope that she would remain speechless until he'd had his say.

"What is wrong with you?" Brandon grumbled without bothering with any polite chitchat. "Hell, girl, you should have that boy tied in knots by now."

"Excuse me, but what *boy* is that?"

"Oh, for heaven's sake, don't play dumb with me. You and Sam. What's taking so long?"

"I wasn't aware that we were on a timetable."

"I'm not going to live forever, you know."

Penny had serious doubts about that. Brandon would stick around as long as he had descendents whose lives he could toy with. "Don't pull that with me," she said. "I'm not falling for it. Besides, why would I marry anyone just because it suited you?"

To her satisfaction, that silenced him.

"You resisting this just because it was my idea?" he inquired finally.

"I am resisting it because Sam Roberts is just about the most stubborn, most bullheaded man I have ever known and he is no more interested in marriage than

I am." Okay, so it was at least half a lie. The truth wouldn't get her off this phone and back to sleep.

Brandon chuckled. "Guess it's just a matter of time, after all."

"I wouldn't hold my breath, if I were you."

"You know he's going back on assignment again," he said slyly. "Something dangerous. Won't even tell me what it is."

Randy hadn't said anything about that at dinner earlier in the week. In fact, he hadn't even hinted that Sam was back at work. Mrs. Farnsworth had told her that the chief had refused to allow Sam back on the job the first time he'd shown up at the station.

Maybe it was a recent development, then. She couldn't deny that the news set off a pang of anxiety. What if it was still too soon? What if he made a costly mistake? Again, for the thousandth time, she saw him on that sidewalk bleeding to death. Her whole body shook at the memory.

Still, Sam had made a decision about the way he wanted to spend his life. It wasn't up to her to try to change him. In fact, her fear was one of the very things standing between them, at least according to him.

"So?" she said to her grandfather, trying desperately to sound disinterested when what she really wanted was to know every detail about where he'd be, who would be his backup, how much danger was involved.

"Doesn't that worry you?" her grandfather demanded, sounding indignant.

"He knows what he's doing," she said, and suddenly realized it was true. She might not like what Sam did for a living, but she'd come to understand not only what it meant to him to try to save those kids, but exactly how good he was at it. Look at what he'd done for Randy. There were probably even more boys she didn't even know about.

It occurred to Penny that it might be a good time to tell him that, just in case something went wrong and she never had another chance. Her heart thudded dully at the thought of what her life would be like without Sam.

But going to Sam with this or anything else was pointless, she realized. If anything was ever to be resolved between them, he had to come to her. It had to be his decision.

"You're not going to try to stop him, are you?" her grandfather asked, clearly disappointed.

"No. It's his decision. It's his life on the line."

"Dammit, girl, don't you see? He doesn't think his life's worth anything."

With an ache in her chest that wouldn't go away, Penny was forced to acknowledge that what her grandfather said was true. Sam had never believed he mattered, not to her, not to anyone.

But how could she prove to him that he was wrong? And how could she do it before it was too late?

"You love him, don't you?" her grandfather asked, his voice gentler.

"Yes."

"Then tell him that."

"I already have. He doesn't believe it will last."

Brandon Halloran sighed heavily. "That boy always did have a head that was hard as a rock. Don't you worry, girl. I'll think of something."

Penny chuckled despite herself. "That's what I'm afraid of."

Before she could try to prevent him from getting involved any more deeply than he already was, her grandfather hung up on her. He didn't even say goodbye. Obviously, he was too busy scheming to worry about the social amenities. That worried her almost as much as thinking of Sam back on the streets again.

Chapter Sixteen

Unable to sleep after her conversation with her grandfather, Penny was up and out of her apartment before dawn. Even so, she found Didi already in the lab, bent over a microscope. She didn't even look up when Penny came in.

"Is this typical of the kind of hours you put in?" Penny asked, pouring herself a cup of the coffee Didi had already brewed.

"I had a brainstorm in the middle of the night and I wanted to get in here early to check it out. What about you?" She glanced at Penny. "Or do I need to ask?"

"What is that supposed to mean?"

"It means you have that wide-awake-all-night-thinking-about-Sam look and the circles under your eyes to go with it."

"Actually, I have that up-all-night-thinking-of-ways-to-stop-my-grandfather-from-meddling look."

"What's he done now?"

"Nothing in the last eight hours or so, but he's scheming. At approximately 12:30 a.m., he promised that he would think of something to get Sam and me back together. I was supposed to be reassured by that."

Didi glanced up from her microscope and regarded Penny wistfully. "You're lucky. I wish somebody would take my social life in hand."

"Trust me, what you need is a social secretary, not a meddling grandfather."

"I'm not so sure about that. At least, he thinks he knows what's right for you. I haven't the vaguest idea what's right for me. I just have people pulling me in different directions."

To her surprise, Penny heard a genuine note of dismay in Didi's voice. She even thought she detected the telltale shimmer of tears in her eyes. Worried by what she saw, Penny pulled up a stool and sat down.

"Okay, talk," she instructed briskly. "You've listened to me enough. It's my turn now. I can't promise advice the caliber of Dear Abby's, but I'll give it my best shot."

Didi shrugged. "There's nothing to say."

Penny rolled her eyes. "For a woman who thinks nothing of dissecting my relationship with Sam, you're awfully tight-lipped about your own feelings. At last count, you'd had three proposals and one big-time proposition for a long-term affair in Tahiti. Or was it Bali? Anyway, all that was in a single week. What you failed to mention was whether you cared about any of the men involved. In fact, I'm not even sure I've ever heard you mention their names. So, what's the deal?"

"Sure, I care," she said readily. "I care about all of them. They're great guys."

"Let me rephrase that," Penny said with exaggerated patience. "Are you in love with any of them?"

"Yes. No." Didi sighed. "Hell, I don't know. Let's not talk about this. The timing on this experiment is critical."

"So's your life." Penny's gaze narrowed. "You're afraid, aren't you?" she said. She recognized all the signs. She'd read them in Sam's expression often enough.

"Sure," Didi confirmed readily enough. "I'm afraid of commitment. My whole life, I've set my own worth based on what other people thought of me. I've turned into an approval junkie. What if I choose one guy and his approval isn't enough? What if I'm always looking for more ways—translate that as affairs—to bolster my self-esteem?"

Penny wondered if Sam faced the same quandary. It would make sense. A boy abandoned by his father, a boy whose mother hadn't cared enough about him to survive the father's leaving, wouldn't that boy always be searching for approval, even as a man?

So, maybe Sam's fears went beyond abandonment. Maybe he simply understood his own constant search for recognition and acceptance and feared that the love of just one woman wouldn't be enough. With every day that passed, she realized she was gaining more insights into the barriers that stood between them. She also realized what tremendous hurdles they were. She prayed for the strength to overcome them.

Looking back at Didi, Penny wanted to shake her. "Don't dare underestimate yourself. Don't you see how much value you have? You're beautiful. You're intelligent. You're funny. Any man would be lucky to have you, just as this lab is blessed to have you on staff. But hearing that from me or anyone else will never be enough. You have to accept it in your gut. You have to believe in yourself."

Penny reached for a notebook and plopped it down on the counter beside her friend. "I want you to stop what you're doing and list every single one of your accomplishments. Then I want you to write down your shortcomings. I guarantee the balance will be all in your favor and it will be right there in black and white for you to study every time you start doubting yourself. You won't need any man's approval."

When she was finished, Didi regarded her curiously. "Was that little speech meant for me or someone else?"

Penny grinned. "You, definitely. But I know one other person who could probably benefit from it."

"Will you tell him?"

"If I ever get the chance." She wouldn't hold her breath while waiting for the opportunity.

That weary sense of resignation didn't take into account her grandfather's determination or how quickly he could mastermind another matchmaking scheme.

It was nearly two the next morning when the phone rang, jarring Sam out of a restless sleep. He knew as he reached for it, that it had to be trouble. At this hour, it always was.

"Sam, is that you?"

He struggled awake. "Granddad Brandon? Is something wrong? Is Mrs. H. okay?"

"Lizzy's fine. Fit as a fiddle. Just thought I'd call to see how you're doing."

"At 2:00 a.m.?"

"Oh," he said without the slightest hint of apology. "I guess I didn't realize how late it was. The time difference always fouls me up."

Sam wasn't buying this vague act for a minute. "What's really on your mind?"

"Mrs. Farnsworth says that boy, Randy, needs a place to stay. Think I should let him move into the house?"

"That's up to you. I think I can guarantee he won't walk off with the silver, if that's worrying you."

"I already gave away the best silver. Your sister was absconding with it piece by piece, first for this holiday, then for that. I finally told her to finish off the set. Anyway, you think this boy'd benefit from being in that house with just Mrs. Farnsworth to look after him?''

"She'd be more family than he's ever had before. If she's willing, I think it would be great."

"I'll give her the go-ahead, then."

"Good. Was there anything else?"

"I wasn't going to mention it," Brandon said, "but..."

Here it comes, Sam thought.

"I'm a little worried about Penny," he said.

Sam sighed. "Don't start with this again."

"No, really. I'm serious. She's planning to drop out of graduate school and leave that job she wanted so badly to move back to California. Why would she want to do that? Getting to Boston meant everything to her. She couldn't wait to get into Harvard. And that job of hers, well, it was a dream come true."

"She's leaving?" Sam said dully, his head beginning to throb. "When?"

"By the end of the week is what she told me the other night."

He snapped fully awake at that. "You mean, Friday? That's the day after tomorrow," he said, astonished by the hastiness of her decision and the speed with which she intended to carry it out.

What the hell was she thinking of? he thought angrily. She couldn't throw out all of her years of work, all of her dreams just because of some ridiculous infatuation she thought she had with him. She'd find somebody else. For that matter, from what he'd seen the other night, she already had. So why would she leave now?

"Did she say why she was going?" he asked cautiously, not sure he wanted to hear the answer. Since Brandon Halloran hadn't started the conversation by cussing him out, Penny apparently hadn't mentioned him among her reasons for packing up and running away.

"Nothing that made a bit of sense," Brandon said vaguely. "I thought maybe you could talk to her, find out what's really going on in that head of hers. She can be downright impulsive sometimes. Maybe you can try to make her see how much she'll regret this."

Though Brandon's evasiveness should have alarmed him, it didn't seem to matter. All that mattered was this gut-deep sense of dread and outrage washing through him.

"Oh, I'll talk to her, all right," Sam said decisively. "She'll move back to California over my dead body."

"I knew I could count on you," Brandon said.

Sam wasn't so incensed by Penny's plans that he missed the smug note in Brandon's voice. Okay, so maybe the old man was scheming again, but he was right to get Sam involved this time. He might very well be the only person on the face of the earth who could make Penny see what a terrible mistake she was making.

He debated waiting until morning to confront her, but decided he'd never sleep another wink, anyway. Besides, he wanted to talk to her while he was still furious. This was one time he didn't intend to give her an inch.

He dragged on his clothes, considered shaving, then dismissed the idea. He doubted she'd notice. It took him considerably less time than the speed limit allowed to get to her apartment. By the time he climbed the stairs, he was ready to wring her neck. He leaned on the buzzer, while pounding on the door.

It took at least five minutes for her to open it. Since she looked wide awake, he guessed it was because she couldn't decide whether or not to let him in.

"Have you lost your mind? It's nearly three in the morning," she told him without stepping aside to let him in.

"Your state of mind is the problem. I just spoke to Granddad Brandon. He told me what you're planning to do and I'll be damned if I'm going to sit by and let it happen."

He bulldozed his way past her and moved to the middle of the living room. "Shut the door."

Her eyes blazed with quick anger. "Excuse me, but this is still my apartment."

He shrugged. "Leave it open, then, and let the neighbors hear everything I have to say. One of them will probably call the cops. Who knows, maybe even Ryan and Jake will be on duty. They'd get a real charge out of getting involved in another one of our little family squabbles."

She closed the door, but she still didn't budge. Sam glanced around the living room for some signs of packing. There were stacks of stuff all over the place, but no boxes. Maybe she just hadn't picked them up yet. Hell, maybe she had a mover coming to pack for her.

"I ought to shake you," he said, glaring at her.

"Exactly what sin am I supposed to have committed now?"

"How long did you dream about going to Harvard?"

"From the time I was sixteen," she said, looking puzzled. "What has that got to do with anything?"

"And what about your job? Do you still like it?"

"I love it."

"Then what the hell is wrong with you? You can't throw it all away and go running back to California just because things haven't worked out for you and me." He walked over to her and put his hands on her shoulders. His voice dropped as he gazed into her startled eyes. "Please, don't make me feel responsible for you giving up your dream."

Penny understood the words. She even understood the vague alarm she thought she detected in his voice. What didn't make sense was why he would be trying to prevent her from doing something she'd never voiced any intention of doing. More important even than that, though, was the genuine dismay evident in his eyes.

Impulsively she reached up and touched his cheek. A shudder swept through him. She could feel it. Suddenly she sensed that they were standing on the edge of a precipice. What she did or said now could make all the difference to their future. Knowing that almost panicked her. She forced herself to go slowly.

"What is this all about?" she asked quietly.

"I don't want you to move back to California."

"Why?"

"Because it would be wrong for you. This is where you belong."

Oh, Sam, she thought miserably. *Why can't you just come out and say it?*

"Why do I belong here?" she asked, determined to make him face what was really upsetting him. However this misunderstanding had begun—and she thought she detected her grandfather's fine hand at work—she intended to make the most of it.

"I grew up in California," she pointed out. "My family's there. Why shouldn't I go back?"

"Now?" he said, clearly exasperated. He shoved his hand through his already mussed hair. "When you're just getting started? Running makes you a coward. Isn't that what you accused me of being?"

"Maybe I had a good teacher," she replied, looking into his eyes. "One of the best, in fact. What's your point?"

"My point is that you belong here." Blue eyes that had turned dark with misery clashed with hers. "Don't go," he said softly.

"Why should I stay here?" she persisted. "Give me one good reason, Sam. Just one."

He looked tormented. He turned away from her, walked to the window and stared outside for what seemed an eternity. Penny ached for him.

With his back still to her, he finally said, "I don't think I could stand it if you left."

Penny's heart thumped unsteadily. She wanted to go to him, to take him in her arms and promise never to leave, but she forced herself to stay where she was.

"Why?" she asked again, knowing she sounded like a child intent on discovering why the sky was blue, the grass green, the stars shiny.

A dry chuckle seemed to be wrenched from him. "You're going to force the words out of me, aren't you?"

"You're asking me to stay in Boston. I think I deserve to know exactly why that matters to you."

"Your dreams are here," he said, turning back to her.

She nodded, allowing herself the beginnings of a smile. "Yes, they are."

"Do those dreams still include me?" The words seemed to have been wrenched from somewhere deep inside him.

"They always have," she admitted. "From the day I met you."

"Then stay," he asked again.

"Why?"

"Because..." He met her gaze, swallowed hard, then tried again. "Because I love you and I want you here with me."

Penny closed her eyes, thrilling to the sensation that those hard-won words sent washing through her. Tears tracked down her cheeks.

"Thank you," she said finally. "Thank you for saying the words. Thank you for finally admitting what you feel."

He still looked uncomfortable with the whole idea, but he didn't go all silent on her.

"I didn't know that was how I felt until tonight when Brandon called and told me you were leaving," he admitted. "I knew that I couldn't let you go. Even five minutes ago, I wasn't sure I knew exactly why keeping you here was so important to me. And I'm still not sure I know exactly what love is, but I know the thought of the emptiness there would be in any life I had without you made me crazy." He smiled slowly. "I guess Randy was right. Men are really lousy at being in touch with their feelings."

She grinned back at him. "Now that you are in touch, aren't you glad?"

He reached for her then and pulled her into his arms. Penny felt the racing of his heart, even as she reveled in his solid strength.

"Frankly, I'm scared spitless," he admitted, holding her tightly. "I don't believe in happily-ever-afters."

"Leave that to me," she told him, sliding both hands up his chest so that she could twine them around his neck. "I'll take care of tomorrow, if you'll concentrate on today." She stood on tiptoe to kiss him. "On this minute." She deepened the kiss. "On this second."

"Like this?"

He grinned and began stripping away her clothes with such slow deliberation that every one of Penny's nerves sizzled with anticipation.

"Exactly like that," she encouraged.

"I'm feeling better about it all the time," he said, his voice husky.

It was only after hours of showing him all the ways she would love him that Penny dared to let him in on how he'd been hoodwinked.

"I was never planning to leave, you know," she said casually, her fingers curled in the mat of hair on his chest.

Hooded blue eyes opened wide. "You weren't?" Then a gleam of understanding lit his eyes. "Your grandfather at work, right?"

"How come when he's meddling, he's mine? You call him Granddad Brandon yourself the rest of the time."

"When he's up to no good, I want no part of him," he said, though he was grinning. "You haven't said, though. Did he make the whole thing up?"

She nodded. "He was getting pretty desperate last time I talked to him," she admitted. "I had no idea he would come up with anything quite so devious, though."

"With his track record? This was pretty tame stuff. In fact, now that I think about it, I'm surprised he didn't try something to motivate you to make the first move. How recently did you talk to him?"

"Just the other night. I didn't hold out a lot of hope for us."

"And he didn't try to manipulate you?" Sam said in amazement.

Penny thought back over the conversation. Most of it had been pretty straightforward. "He did mention that you'd gone back to work. He suggested you might be a little careless, since you didn't place much value on your own life. He wanted me to try to stop you."

Sam regarded her intently. "You didn't believe him?"

"I believed that you might not think people care about you, even though there's tons of evidence to the contrary, but I didn't for a moment believe you'd be careless. You're too good a cop. And I refused to interfere."

He took a deep breath. "That's something we should talk about. I could give it up, take that job at Halloran he's always offering me," he said.

Penny heard the anguish in his voice and knew how difficult it had been for him to make the offer. She pulled out of his arms and drew herself up onto her knees. Gazing into his eyes, she took his face in her hands. "You don't have to do that for me."

"I don't want you terrified every time I walk out the door to go to work. I don't want you caught up in the ugliness the way you were with Tank."

"I can handle it," she reassured him, forcing the brave words out. "The only thing I couldn't handle would be losing you because I've tried to turn you into somebody else. You wouldn't be happy. You'd resent it and me. Besides, with you on the job, maybe one day there won't be so many guys like Tank on the street anyway."

Sam's hands closed over hers and brought them to his lips. "I love you," he said quietly.

And this time, to Penny's joy, he didn't stumble over the words at all.

Epilogue

Brandon Halloran stood in the hospital hallway gazing raptly at the baby who was squalling his head off in the bassinet right down front in the crowded nursery. The nurse had pointed him out, but Brandon was convinced he would have recognized him anywhere.

"Looks just like you," Lizzy observed.

He gazed down at his beloved wife and saw the twinkle in her eyes. "He is a handsome little devil, isn't he?"

"I was referring to his big mouth."

He scowled at her affectionately. "Hush, woman. That's my great-grandbaby you're talking about."

"And mine," she reminded him tartly. Then her voice softened. "Oh, Brandon, he really is precious, isn't he? Have you ever seen a baby as cute?"

Brandon heard the chuckles behind him and turned to find Sam and Penny watching them, their eyes sparkling with tolerant amusement.

"Even though it's barely dawn, we thought we'd find you here," Penny said, hugging them both. "Couldn't you even come to say hello to the new mother first? Everyone else has gone home now."

"Thanks to your bad planning, we took that blasted red-eye flight. I'm getting too old to fly all night and still be sociable in the morning." His gaze narrowed. "What made you think we'd be down here? How'd you even know we were back in town?"

Penny laughed. "Are you kidding? We've had minute-by-minute reports from the second your plane took off from Los Angeles, primarily because that's how frequently you called. Whoever put telephones into airplanes obviously had you in mind."

She gazed up at her husband. "How many times did he check in with your sister?"

"Six at last count," Sam reported to Brandon's chagrin. "Jason unplugged the phone."

"And with Kevin and Lacey?"

Sam shot him a grin. "I believe they stopped answering after the first ten calls."

Penny nodded. "Sounds about right. Add that to the half dozen calls fielded by the nursing staff and the one that actually got put through to the delivery room and I'd say you didn't miss one single minute of

my labor. By the way, the doctor says he's charging
extra for having to put up with your consultation. He
wasn't overjoyed by all your questions about his
qualifications, either.''

Brandon took the taunting in stride. He loved the
sass the women in his life gave him. The men, too, for
that matter. The fact that they still indulged in so
much affectionate teasing made him feel alive. Some
men his age were all but ignored by their families.
Knowing that would never happen to him filled him
with joy. He gave thanks for it every day of his life.

He frowned at his granddaughter. "If you hadn't
gone and had him so blasted fast, I'd have been here
before the end," he informed her huffily. "You always were in a rush."

"It didn't seem fast to me," she protested. "And,
frankly, I wasn't about to let it drag on just to suit
your timetable. If you wanted to be in on the delivery, you should have come back a week ago when I
warned you I thought he was going to be early."

Brandon shot an I-told-you-so glance at his wife
and caught Lizzy lifting an imploring gaze toward
heaven. That look was mighty familiar. She often
asked for help in putting up with his shenanigans.
Made a big deal of it, in fact, but he guessed she
wouldn't have him any other way.

"Don't get him started on that, please," she begged
Penny. "It's all my fault. I told him first babies were
almost never early and that labor always took a long
time. He grumbled at me from the minute the call
came in and never let up until we touched down in

Boston. Don't blame me if he takes up residence in your guest room from your seventh month on next time."

Brandon leaned on the cane that more and more seemed to be a necessity since he'd broken his hip in an absurd skiing accident in Switzerland the previous winter. Whoever heard of putting a tree smack in the middle of a ski run? At any rate, he was just glad it had been him and not Lizzy. She was never going to let him forget it as it was. She had told him they had no business trying to learn to ski at their age. He'd figured they didn't have any time to waste. He wanted to try everything he'd missed out on over the years. He might even take up roller-blading one of these days.

But no matter how far they traveled or how many adventures they shared, coming home to family was still what he liked best. He thought he could relax a little now that his favorite granddaughter and that rapscallion husband of hers had finally settled down. Getting them married had required the last of his matchmaking skills. He thought maybe it was time to retire from the meddling business . . . at least until the next generation was a little older and needed some sage advice.

He gazed into the nursery at the squalling baby again and his heart swelled with pride and a sense of accomplishment that wasn't rightly his to feel. "You named him yet?"

Penny and Sam exchanged a look.

"There was never any doubt about it," Sam said.

Brandon regarded the pair of them with tears in his eyes as he anticipated the answer. He hadn't dared to hope they would honor him this way.

"With your permission, we'd like to call him Brandon Halloran Roberts," said the fine young man Brandon had always thought of as one of his own.

Penny reached out and squeezed his hand. "We love you, Grandfather," she said.

His throat clogged with emotion. "Nothing could make me happier than having this baby as my name-sake," he told them. "I just pray he'll have half the life I've had."

His gaze went to Lizzy and turned gentle. "And some small measure of the love," he added. "If he has that, his life will be rich, indeed."

Sam slid his arm around Penny's waist and re-garded Brandon with all the strength and determina-tion Brandon had always known he possessed. It was Penny, though, who had given him the ability to see it in himself.

"We'll see to it that he does," Sam promised. "He's got a father who's finally learned what love and family are all about."

Sam's gaze settled on his wife then and Brandon could see the depth of emotion these two shared. It had been a long time coming, but it was the kind of bond that would last through all time, just as his had with Lizzy.

With his own heart overflowing with joy, Brandon reached for his wife's hand.

"We've been blessed, Lizzy."

She reached up and touched his weathered old cheek. The caress still had the power to stir him.

"Twice blessed," she reminded him. "It's a legacy we can leave to all the generations of Hallorans to come."

* * * * *

COUNTDOWN
Lindsay McKenna

Sergeant Joe Donnally knew being a marine
meant putting lives on the line—and after a tragic
loss, he vowed never to love again. Yet here was
Annie Yellow Horse, the passionate, determined
woman who challenged him to feel long-dormant
emotions. But Joe had to conquer past demons before
declaring his love....

MEN OF COURAGE

It's a special breed of men who defy death and fight
for right! Salute their bravery while sharing their lives
and loves!

These are courageous men you'll love and tender
stories you'll cherish...available in June, only from
Silhouette Special Edition!

MILLION DOLLAR SWEEPSTAKES (III)

No purchase necessary. To enter, follow the directions published. Method of entry may vary. For eligibility, entries must be received no later than March 31, 1996. No liability is assumed for printing errors, lost, late or misdirected entries. Odds of winning are determined by the number of eligible entries distributed and received. Prizewinners will be determined no later than June 30, 1996.

Sweepstakes open to residents of the U.S. (except Puerto Rico), Canada, Europe and Taiwan who are 18 years of age or older. All applicable laws and regulations apply. Sweepstakes offer void wherever prohibited by law. Values of all prizes are in U.S. currency. This sweepstakes is presented by Torstar Corp., its subsidiaries and affiliates, in conjunction with book, merchandise and/or product offerings. For a copy of the Official Rules send a self-addressed, stamped envelope (WA residents need not affix return postage) to: MILLION DOLLAR SWEEPSTAKES (III) Rules, P.O. Box 4573, Blair, NE 68009, USA.

EXTRA BONUS PRIZE DRAWING

No purchase necessary. The Extra Bonus Prize will be awarded in a random drawing to be conducted no later than 5/30/96 from among all entries received. To qualify, entries must be received by 3/31/96 and comply with published directions. Drawing open to residents of the U.S. (except Puerto Rico), Canada, Europe and Taiwan who are 18 years of age or older. All applicable laws and regulations apply; offer void wherever prohibited by law. Odds of winning are dependent upon number of eligibile entries received. Prize is valued in U.S. currency. The offer is presented by Torstar Corp., its subsidiaries and affiliates in conjunction with book, merchandise and/or product offering. For a copy of the Official Rules governing this sweepstakes, send a self-addressed, stamped envelope (WA residents need not affix return postage) to: Extra Bonus Prize Drawing Rules, P.O. Box 4590, Blair, NE 68009, USA.

SWP-S594

DAUGHTER OF THE BRIDE
Christine Flynn

Abby Lawrence's dreams of love were fulfilled in
a night of passion with childhood sweetheart
Marc Maddox. Their unchecked emotion wasn't
without consequences, though Abby had chosen to
brave it alone. Now, years later, Abby's secret was
threatened—jeopardizing her loving reunion
with Marc....

Don't miss Christine Flynn's
DAUGHTER OF THE BRIDE, available in June!

She's friend, wife, mother—she's you! And beside
each Special Woman stands a wonderfully *special*
man. It's a celebration of our heroines—and the men
who become part of their lives.

Don't miss **THAT SPECIAL WOMAN!** each month—
from some of your special authors!

TSW694

IT'S OUR 1000TH SILHOUETTE ROMANCE, AND WE'RE CELEBRATING!

JOIN US FOR A SPECIAL COLLECTION OF LOVE STORIES BY AUTHORS YOU'VE LOVED FOR YEARS, AND NEW FAVORITES YOU'VE JUST DISCOVERED. JOIN THE CELEBRATION...

April
REGAN'S PRIDE by Diana Palmer
MARRY ME AGAIN by Suzanne Carey

May
THE BEST IS YET TO BE by Tracy Sinclair
CAUTION: BABY AHEAD by Marie Ferrarella

June
THE BACHELOR PRINCE by Debbie Macomber
A ROGUE'S HEART by Laurie Paige

July
IMPROMPTU BRIDE by Annette Broadrick
THE FORGOTTEN HUSBAND by Elizabeth August

SILHOUETTE ROMANCE...VIBRANT, FUN AND EMOTIONALLY RICH! TAKE ANOTHER LOOK AT US! AND AS PART OF THE CELEBRATION, READERS CAN RECEIVE A FREE GIFT!

YOU'LL FALL IN LOVE ALL OVER AGAIN WITH SILHOUETTE ROMANCE!

Silhouette®

CEL1000

Also available by popular author

SHERRYL WOODS

Silhouette Special Edition®

#09669	MY DEAREST CAL	$3.25	☐
#09713	JOSHUA AND THE COWGIRL	$3.29	☐
#09769	*LOVE	$3.39	☐
#09775	*HONOR	$3.39	☐
#09781	*CHERISH	$3.39	☐
#09823	*KATE'S VOW	$3.50	☐
#09855	*A DARING VOW	$3.50	☐

*Vows miniseries

Silhouette Desire®

#05601	NEXT TIME...FOREVER	$2.50	☐
#05620	FEVER PITCH	$2.50	☐
#05708	DREAM MENDER	$2.89	☐

(limited quantities available on certain titles)

TOTAL AMOUNT	$
POSTAGE & HANDLING	$
($1.00 for one book, 50¢ for each additional)	
APPLICABLE TAXES**	$
TOTAL PAYABLE	$

(Send check or money order—please do not send cash)

To order, complete this form and send it, along with a check or money order for the total above, payable to Silhouette Books, to: **In the U.S.:** 3010 Walden Avenue, P.O. Box 9077, Buffalo, NY 14269-9077; **In Canada:** P.O. Box 636, Fort Erie, Ontario, L2A 5X3.

Name:_____

Address:_____City:_____

State/Prov.:_____Zip/Postal Code:_____

**New York residents remit applicable sales taxes.
Canadian residents remit applicable GST and provincial taxes.

SWBACK2

▼ *Silhouette* ®
TM